It wasn't until Sam cleaned her plate that she realized Dad was even quieter than usual. Then he left the table without dessert.

"What's up?" Sam asked when she and Gram were alone.

Gram looked down and shook her head. "Gracious, I thought your dad would talk with you about this, but I see he's left it for me."

"Left what?" Sam didn't like the careful way Gram was talking.

"Well, you've a right to know." Gram met Sam's eyes. "Your dad talked with Dr. Scott today."

Glen Scott was the levelheaded veterinarian who was a favorite among the local ranchers for all equine problems. Something must be wrong with one of the horses, but Sam couldn't bear to ask which one.

"Dr. Scott told Wyatt that those mustangs up at Willow Springs are in big trouble." Gram had to clear her throat before she could continue. Sam was still feeling grateful that nothing was wrong with the River Bend horses when Gram added, "The BLM wants to put them down."

Read all the books in the PHANTOM STALLION *series:*

Phantom Stallion

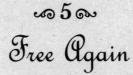

∽ 5 ∽

Free Again

TERRI FARLEY

AVON BOOKS

An Imprint of HarperCollins*Publishers*

Library of Congress Catalog Card Number:
2002091785
ISBN 0-06-441089-7

First Avon edition, 2003

❖

Visit us on the World Wide Web!
www.harperchildrens.com

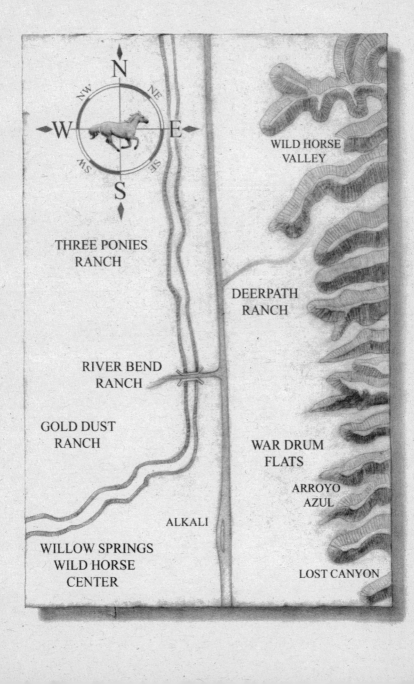

Chapter One &

SAMANTHA FORSTER stepped off the school bus and into an icy wind that hinted snow wasn't far away. She zipped up her blue fleece jacket, plunged her hands deep into her pockets, and shivered.

Her best friend, Jen, who usually kept her company on the long walk home, had stayed after school for an advanced math review. The weather wasn't so bad that Gram would drive to the bus stop to pick Sam up. So Sam trudged toward River Bend Ranch alone.

She looked over her shoulder and let her eyes search the Calico Mountains. Just for a minute, she told herself, because of course it was a waste of time.

Up there lay the Phantom's hidden valley. The clouds scudding overhead made the mountains look as dark as Sam's hopes. The magnificent silver mustang wanted nothing to do with her, because she'd betrayed him. Sam felt as if a cold metal ball had lodged where her heart should be. If only she could apologize.

She hadn't betrayed the Phantom, not really, but all his equine mind could know was that she hadn't been there when he needed her.

And now he was nowhere to be found. For weeks, she'd watched the La Charla River at night. Her eyes had searched War Drum Flats as the school bus drove by. And every day she stared at the mountains. Not once had she seen the pale, faraway shape of the Phantom.

Sam hoisted the straps of her backpack and sighed. She wanted to visit the stallion's haven. She imagined herself riding down the dark secret tunnel and emerging into the sunlight to be greeted by a soft nicker that would mean the Phantom had forgiven her for being human.

But that wouldn't work. He had to come to her. Because he hadn't, Sam was afraid the stallion had finally lost faith in people. Even her.

She was so intent on the mountain, she didn't notice the three horses in front of her until one snorted.

Two paints and a bay clustered together, shoulder to shoulder, tails to the wind.

She knew right away they weren't mustangs. The bay's nose showed a rubbed place from years of wearing a halter. The tap dancing sound of their hooves said there might be shoes on their overgrown hooves. They jostled against each other to get a better look at Sam.

"Who do you belong to, poor babies?"

Three sets of ears pricked farther forward. One of the paints was mostly white. He cocked his head to the side before taking a few cautious steps toward Sam. The others followed. They kept edging forward until they were only about six feet away.

Sam knew all of River Bend's horses, and most horses from the Three Ponies and Gold Dust ranches, but she didn't know these. Since this was open range, they could have come from almost anywhere. Many ranchers only fenced a few acres of their land, and the Bureau of Land Management didn't fence any.

Impatient for attention, the bay pawed and nickered.

"You're hungry, aren't you?" Sam crooned to the horse. Wind fluttered the bay's thickening winter coat, and she thought she could see the outline of ribs.

A quick look at the other two horses showed Sam they were just as neglected.

Sam's cheeks heated with anger. Whoever owned these animals ought to live the same way the horses did. Let the owner go without shelter, meals, and shoes that fit, and see how he liked it.

"I have treats." Sam's singsong voice drew the horses closer. "Granola bars for everyone."

She eased her backpack off each shoulder and let

it down to the desert floor. She crouched beside it, sliding the zipper open quietly, so the horses wouldn't be frightened and bolt. She needn't have bothered. They were too curious to go anywhere.

"I knew these would come in handy." Sam retrieved four foil-wrapped granola bars from her backpack.

Although Gram had learned that Sam wasn't hungry in the morning, she never gave up. She kept offering bacon and eggs, biscuits and gravy, but Sam was satisfied with cereal. So Gram made her take a granola bar, every day, just in case her stomach began growling before lunchtime.

"Honey and oats," Sam announced. She broke the first bar into three pieces. Before she had a chance to toss them to the horses, the mostly white paint shoved past the others and began nuzzling her hand. "Greedy guts," Sam called the horse, but the paint just tossed his head in delight.

She shared the food among them. Although the granola bars had lots of sugar and probably weren't too nutritious for the horses, Sam didn't worry. She might be the first to consider the horses' health for a long time.

They chewed, then sniffed, whiskers brushing the desert. As the horses searched for crumbs, Sam checked them for brands. She didn't see any, though the marks could be hidden under their shaggy hair.

"We're going to do something about this," she told

them. "And the first thing to do is get you a real meal."

Should she challenge these horses' owners? Sam didn't wonder long. She'd failed to keep the Phantom safe, but she wouldn't fail these horses who'd walked right up and asked for her help.

Like three big dogs, the horses followed Sam. She tried not to imagine what Dad would say when he saw them.

Dad made lots of rules. His strictest rule was that everyone on the ranch worked and every animal earned its feed. River Bend horses worked the same long days as the cowboys. Gram cooked and cleaned in addition to being the ranch bookkeeper and Dad's business partner. Sam's chores were more than a formality. Without her help, Gram and Dad would be working long after sundown. Even Blaze, the dog, could herd cattle and sound the alarm when strangers neared the ranch.

"But all kids bring home strays, don't they?" Sam asked the horses.

They didn't answer, so she didn't mention that the River Bend Ranch already had two mustangs that weren't working. At least the BLM paid Dad to keep them. Popcorn and Dark Sunshine were part of the Horse and Rider Protection program. HARP paired mustangs that had been adopted, then abused or neglected, with troubled girls. Together, the girls and mustangs recovered and learned to trust each other.

But Sam didn't think Dad would sympathize with three tame horses looking for a handout.

On the other hand, though it was overcast and gray, it wasn't near sundown. Dad was probably still out on the range.

At the edge of the La Charla River, the horses stopped and drank, but not deeply.

"Someone's watering you, at least," Sam said.

But the horses wouldn't cross the bridge that led to the ranch.

"C'mon," she said. "We've got great hay in here, and maybe I could find you a little grain."

Sam smooched to the horses, but they just tossed tangled forelocks away from their eyes and watched her.

She clapped her hands softly, trying to coax them into the ranch yard. Her move was a mistake.

The three horses backed up, then trotted away from her and the ranch.

Frustrated, Sam crossed the bridge and walked toward the house. Blaze bounded out to meet her.

"You missed all the fun," Sam said to the Border collie. He lifted his head, testing the wind, then pricked his ears toward the bridge. The horses' scent must have lingered.

The captive mustangs had caught the scent, too.

Excited by the prospect of company, Dark Sunshine and Popcorn were galloping laps around the ten-acre pasture. The cow ponies were out on the range working, but the mustangs enjoyed their herd of two. Popcorn's long white legs carried him ahead of the small buckskin.

"Sorry," Sam called to the horses. "They were too shy to come meet you."

Sam looked hard, trying to see any signs that Dark Sunshine was in foal. She didn't see anything, but the vet had said the mare would give birth to the Phantom's colt or filly sometime in late spring.

The screen door slammed as Gram came out on the porch. Sam gave Blaze's ears a hurried rumple, then walked faster as she neared the house.

Something had to be done about those neglected horses.

"What's got the animals so excited?" Gram asked.

"Three horses followed me home."

Gram peered past Sam, saw nothing, then chuckled. "Lands, don't ask if you can keep them." Clearly, she thought Sam was joking.

"Really," Sam insisted, but the horses were long gone and no dust marked their passing.

"Why don't you come have a little something to eat?" Gram held the screen door wide. "Today I stripped the tree of its last peaches and made a cobbler. I'm wondering if these cold nights hurt the fruit." Gram's apron smelled of cinnamon as she gave Sam a hug. "We'll both have some and you can tell me all about these tagalong horses."

Sam had told her tale and started upstairs to

change out of her school clothes when Gram called after her.

"You said two *paint* horses, didn't you?" Gram didn't give Sam time to answer. "You know, Trudy Allen always fancied paint horses, but I figured she sold them along with all of her cattle."

"Who?" Sam came halfway back down the stairs.

"You must remember Mrs. Allen." Gram wore a troubled frown, and suddenly Sam did remember.

Chills scurried down her arms like a bunch of freezing-footed lizards. Sam thought of toadstools, bubbling cauldrons, and Hansel and Gretel. Yes, she remembered Mrs. Allen.

When she and Jake Ely were little, they'd been petrified of her. Jake and Sam had been friends forever. And for just as long, he'd acted braver and tougher because he was two and a half years older. But Jake's fearlessness had faded—and he'd stayed close to his big brothers—whenever he rode onto Mrs. Allen's property.

Mrs. Allen's lavender Victorian house was surrounded by roses and an iron fence with uprights like twisted spears. It sat in the middle of Deerpath Ranch, looking creepy and out of place. The house didn't fit into the ranching community any more than Mrs. Allen did.

"Is she still alive?" Sam blurted.

"Samantha Anne, I should wash out your mouth with soap!" Gram jerked loose the ties on her apron and held it crumpled in one hand. "Of course she's still alive. Trudy Allen is about the same age I am."

"Sorry, Gram." Sam wouldn't have believed anyone except Gram. Mrs. Allen had always looked a hundred years old. "She just—" Sam stopped, and Gram's expression said it was a good thing. "I am sorry."

"You're about to be sorrier, young lady," Gram said. "Don't bother changing our of your school clothes. We need to see if those are Trudy's horses."

"But it's awfully cold—"

"What a nice opportunity to wear your suede jacket with the sheepskin lining." Gram rolled down the sleeves she'd turned up while cooking.

Sam didn't explain that her chills weren't from the weather. She thought of another excuse. "I have chores and homework—"

"That's the nice thing about work. It always waits for you." Gram nodded as she buttoned her cuffs. "Now, I'll get a jar of peach jam to take along, just to be neighborly."

"Gram, you didn't see those horses. If you had, you wouldn't want to be nice."

"I'm not going to be, Samantha. You are."

You are. The words echoed as Sam stared. Gram's smile looked a little too sweet.

"You don't mean . . . ." Sam spoke slowly. If she'd misunderstood, she didn't want to give Gram any ideas. "You're sending *me* out there? Just me?"

It had been bad enough when she thought they were going together. She might be thirteen and a freshman in high school, but Sam did not want to go to Mrs. Allen's spook house all alone.

"Goodness, Samantha, I'm not sending you to Mars. Deerpath Ranch is no farther than the Gold Dust, and you ride over to see Jen all the time. It's just in another direction. A direction" — Gram's tone turned sympathetic—"you've been staring in quite a lot lately."

Sam nodded. Deerpath Ranch lay between River Bend and the Calico Mountains. The very paths it had been named for were shared by the mustangs. The Phantom might even consider the ranch his territory.

Sam felt torn. "I don't care how far it is. Ace can use the run, but—"

"There you go, then," Gram said.

Gram hustled back toward the kitchen and Sam followed at her heels, trying to think of another excuse. Anything was better than the embarrassing truth.

Gram was reaching into a cupboard for jam when she turned so suddenly that Sam nearly bumped into her. Gram's arms were full and a frown line appeared between her eyebrows. But it was the way she studied Sam that told her Gram had remembered. "Maybe Trudy felt abandoned when her kids went away to college and never moved back home, but that's been ten years, now. And when her husband died, soon after, Trudy did turn a bit private and peculiar," Gram admitted. "But, Sam, please tell me you don't still believe she's a witch."

Chapter Two ⁓

ACE RAN INTO THE WIND and Sam leaned forward, cheek pressed to the gelding's warm neck. She squinted against the whipping of his coarse black mane. With her eyes half closed, she could imagine the blurry world around her held the Phantom. Maybe he was running behind her, long legs sweeping forward again and again until he could catch up and gallop beside her, matching strides with Ace.

But she and Ace were alone. She felt the smooth sway and shift of Ace's muscles as he veered around rocks and sagebrush. Only four hooves pounded the desert floor.

Sam told herself it didn't matter. The Phantom would come to her when he was ready. For now, it was enough to hold close to Ace—who, she was sure, wouldn't have been running with such speed if he'd known each stride carried them closer to Mrs. Allen's haunted house.

Sensing the change in her mood, Ace slowed to a lope, then a hammering trot. Sam didn't correct him. She was too busy looking at the remains of Deerpath Ranch.

Although much of the land was fenced, no cattle or horses would have trouble escaping.

"You could step right over that, couldn't you, boy?" Sam asked Ace. So could the three shaggy horses she'd seen this afternoon.

The fence posts had loosened with the changing seasons and no one had dug fresh holes or reset the posts. The barbed wire strands had stretched with age and the crossing of animals.

Now the posts and rusty wire bowed with each gust of wind. Ace's ears flicked toward the rasp of wire on wood, but he trotted on.

The hay fields lay abandoned except for one piece of farm machinery. The wheeled contraption sat where it had stopped. Unsure what it was, Sam rose in her stirrups to study it. She still couldn't tell, but judging from the ripped upholstery on the driver's seat and the field mouse nest built in the seat's cottony stuffing, it had been there for a while.

Sam urged Ace toward the fenced lane leading to the house. He shied at something moving up ahead. It was a coyote. His gray coat matched the desert shadows. If not for his tawny face tipped to one side with curiosity, she might have missed him. The coyote's front paws shifted as he stopped, considered horse and rider, then bounded over the fence and off toward the foothills of the Calico Mountains.

"He's gone," Sam told Ace. Neither of them was afraid of coyotes, but this one had appeared out of nowhere.

Nonsense, Sam told herself. It's dusk. Coyotes blend in with their background and the evening had turned a hazy purple-beige.

Head tossing, Ace turned onto the lane. In memory, the lane was soft and powdery. The soil had shown each hoofprint. She must have been pretty little when she'd traveled it last, since she remembered wanting to climb off her pony to dig in the dirt. Now the lane was carpeted with weeds, as if no one ever came this way.

Suddenly, Sam saw the house. Its front door faced her and its back was turned on the hillside. Everything about the house seemed pointed: its zigzag roofline, the spear-shaped bars in the fence, and the triangular sign that warned KEEP OUT.

Once, people had probably considered the house elegant. Sam remembered a rose garden and an ornate iron fence. The house was the last piece of civilization before the open range. But it wasn't elegant or civilized now.

Twilight had turned its lavender paint to gray. One of its window shutters flapped in the wind. The shutter struck the house, sounding as if someone was knocking. The other shutters hung like broken wings.

A tumbleweed bounded across the yard in front of Ace, to join the others mounded up against the barn.

The place was a shambles.

Chills raced down Sam's arms as she realized she might have been right, after all. Maybe Mrs. Allen's horses were wandering, hungry, across the countryside because she *had* died.

Sam would not go into the house to find out. Gram wouldn't want her to. But Gram would expect her to knock and leave the jars of jam.

Sam took one deep breath. Then another. She tried to work up the nerve to dismount, open the gate in the iron fence, and walk through. Such bravery stayed out of reach until a loud series of welcoming neighs made Sam jump.

She turned in her saddle, searching for horses. She saw a small corral next to the barn. The connecting door swayed on creaky hinges, but there were no horses in sight.

Then she spotted a large square corral. There stood the two paints and the old bay. They *were* Deerpath horses.

Still side by side, they waited in the corral. There wasn't a blade of grass or a wisp of straw to be seen. The gate was wide open, creaking in the wind on hinges in need of oil.

Ace returned their greeting with a nicker and Sam patted his neck. "I'll feed them in a minute, Ace. I promise."

She would, too, even if she had to search that ramshackle barn in the dark.

Determination to help the horses made Sam hurry. She swung down from Ace's saddle and looped the reins over one of the spikes in the iron fence.

She couldn't help staring at the spike, even though it wasn't as sharp as she recalled. How old had she been—six or seven?—when she and Jake had walked up to the house, hand in hand like Hansel and Gretel? And what had they been doing here?

Sam didn't remember. She only recalled how they'd worried that Mrs. Allen's dogs might leap but not clear the fence. She tried to remember the dogs. What breed were they? Dad had called them bull-dogs, hadn't he? Someone else, maybe Dallas, had called them devil dogs.

Her memory might be hazy, but she knew they'd panted, snarled, and had fangs to slash a child's tender legs. What else did a kid need to know?

Just the same, she and Jake had shivered at the idea of dogs impaled on the gruesome fence.

Looking up at the house, Sam saw a twist of smoke rising from the chimney. Mrs. Allen wasn't dead.

Sam stood directly in front of the gate.

Get a grip, she scolded herself. How could she be afraid of a little old lady?

She lifted the latch on the iron gate. *Clank*.

The sound set off rapid barks from inside the

house. If Mrs. Allen's dogs had lived this long, they were tough little creatures.

Holding a jam jar in each hand, Sam marched up the path and onto the front porch. She juggled the jam to one arm, then knocked. And waited.

"Get away from my door!" a scratchy voice ordered.

"Mrs. Allen? It's Samantha—"

"What do you want?"

Sam didn't like shouting at a closed door, but she had no choice. "My grandmother—Grace Forster?— sent you some peach jam."

"You tell Grace I don't need charity!" The voice was forceful but weary.

Sam released half a sigh. At least Mrs. Allen admitted she knew Gram.

"Mrs. Allen? Gram's just being neighborly."

Rustling came from inside. Was the old lady watching through the peephole or getting ready to free the dogs?

"Leave it, then, and get off my porch!" There was a thump as something inside struck the floor.

Sam squatted, keeping her eyes on the door as she put the jars down. It would have been so easy to obey Mrs. Allen's order to scat, but she didn't.

"Your horses are hungry." Sam's voice came out wavering, so she cleared her throat and tried again. "Mrs. Allen, your horses were all the way over by River Bend Ranch looking for food."

"I never neglect my horses."

Sam retreated a step. Mrs. Allen's voice suddenly sounded stronger. Sam's heart pounded, warning her to run.

"I'm telling the truth," Sam insisted. Walking backward, she took the first step off the porch. "They're hungry."

"Get off my property or you'll be sorry!"

Claws scrabbled against the wooden door and the dogs growled. If they got out, she couldn't run or they'd chase her. Swirling around her ankles, they might slash at Ace.

Suddenly Sam knew what to do.

"I'm going!" She ran down the path, swung into the saddle, and turned Ace away from the ranch.

The gelding hesitated, tossing his head and resisting the pressure of her knees. Mustangs craved the safety of the herd. Ace didn't want to leave the horses in the pen, but with the dogs barking louder and Mrs. Allen yelling, Sam made him mind.

"Git!" Sam nudged Ace with her heels and twirled the ends of her reins where he could see them. With a snort, he leaped in the direction she'd chosen.

Sam urged Ace up one of the trails snaking over the hillside. A narrow track split off the main path and curved around behind the house. Sam took it. She didn't ride fast and she didn't look back. Mrs. Allen might be mad enough to follow her, but she hadn't sounded strong enough.

As soon as she'd ridden out of sight, Sam drew rein and settled in to wait. With the flat of her hand, she felt Ace's neck. He was hot, but not wet.

"Good boy," she praised him, but Ace shook his head and the leather reins made a slapping sound. The gelding was mad because she'd made him leave the others. "You'll see them again in a little while, Ace. There's no way I'd let horses go hungry."

This was going to get her in trouble.

Sam should've been home by now. It was past dinnertime and it was a school night. Ever since she'd earned a C in algebra for the first-quarter grading period, Gram and Dad had harassed her every night about her homework. But she had to feed those horses.

Good sense told her to go home and get Dad or Gram to drive back over. The Big Dipper showed faintly in the ink-blue sky and the wind was rising again. She was cold. She had every reason to leave, but she wanted to do this on her own.

Admit it, Sam told herself, *you want to be a hero*.

She'd done a lot of things lately that *she* thought were heroic—like helping free the Phantom from Karla Starr's rodeo and rescuing Dark Sunshine from the wild horse rustlers. But did Dad and Gram think she was brave? No. They agreed with Brynna Olson, manager of the BLM's wild horse corrals, who said Sam was foolhardy.

"What's the difference between brave and fool-hardy, Ace? Do you know?"

The gelding stamped. He didn't care about heroism. He cared about hay. His dinnertime had passed, too.

"Soon," Sam whispered to her horse.

She'd heard the door open twice, but Mrs. Allen hadn't emerged. Was the old lady looking for her? Probably. And the only way she could be sure Mrs. Allen wouldn't set the dogs on her was if she waited until it was completely dark, when she couldn't be seen.

All at once, lights came on in Mrs. Allen's house. They shone through an upstairs window that was round and set with stained glass.

Upstairs. Maybe she was getting ready for bed. Old people went to bed early, didn't they?

"I bet she's had *her* dinner," Sam said to Ace. It wasn't fair for Mrs. Allen to leave those three horses hungry.

Once more Ace stamped and swished his tail. Then his body twisted, and she felt a hump in his back. Ace was sick and tired of waiting. He might start bucking if she didn't get this show on the road.

"Knock it off, boy." Sam gave a little tug on the reins, but she knew she couldn't wait much longer.

If Ace decided he really wanted to throw her, he would. She still wasn't a skilled rider. And she didn't want to be stranded afoot out here. Mrs. Allen might not be a witch, but . . .

All of a sudden, Sam knew she was being watched. She froze. That's what rabbits did. They went still, hoping to fade into their environment. But she was no rabbit. She was sitting on a big brown horse. Nothing could hide her.

Something moved.

Sam kicked Ace into action. He trotted a few steps before she looked back.

Nothing. And Ace wasn't afraid, just restless.

With her pulse still pounding like a woodpecker's tap, she pulled Ace to a stop. Something had moved on the hillside behind her. It was just too dark to see *what*.

"Duh," she mocked herself. "Deerpath Ranch . . . d'you think it might have been a deer?"

She could make out only rocks and sagebrush. Dirt crunched, but why should she be afraid? Nothing could hide there. Oh, another coyote, maybe. And there among piñon pines, twisted by wind and lack of water, maybe a bobcat. But she was too big for a cat to stalk.

Below, a door creaked open again. Good. Mrs. Allen must be coming out to feed her horses. After she'd finished, Sam would ride home. Maybe she wouldn't be grounded for life.

Ace strained against the bit, ready to explode, and suddenly Sam felt what her horse had sensed.

The creature in the dark had moved closer.

Chapter Three ❧

At first, Sam thought the figure in the darkness was a ghost.

Pale in the moonless night, he looked like the smudged chalk portrait of a horse.

"Zanzibar." Sam whispered her secret name for the Phantom. At last, he'd come to her. Her heart opened with gladness.

The stallion's windblown outline changed as she watched. He moved farther off, mane lifting like silver flame. Her voice had always soothed him before. Not this time. Though his eyes were hidden by darkness, Sam could tell the silver stallion was braced for an attack.

His beauty and speed made men hunt him. He couldn't trust humankind anymore. Not even her.

But he'd come this close. Surely that was a sign their broken friendship could be mended. She'd give him a minute to remember how he'd liked the sound of her voice. Then she'd try again.

Ace didn't nicker a greeting or try to touch noses with his old herd leader. Instead, he danced in place, fighting the reins. Sam gathered them, but it wasn't enough. Her shoulder joints protested as Ace flexed his neck against her hold.

The Phantom's hooves crunched rocks and dry dirt as he launched himself farther off. She could still see him, shifting with uncertainty. He had every reason to run, but she tried once more to make him stay.

Just as she took a breath, Ace rose on his hind legs.

"Zanzibar, don't go!" Sam's voice soared with the gelding's movements.

Afraid she'd fall, Sam loosened her reins and jammed her weight forward. Ace came down.

Even before his forefeet touched, Sam saw the Phantom dash through a thicket of sagebrush. Her voice had frightened him, not soothed him.

The brush rustled as the stallion pushed through. She could still see his head and neck. Thin branches snapped and he vanished around a bend in the trail. A rock rolled, but she could see nothing.

For a moment, the wind held its breath. If Ace weren't still trembling with excitement, Sam might have wondered if the Phantom had ever really been there.

Down below, a moving light caught Sam's eyes. A

flashlight beam swept back and forth across the dirt yard between the house and the corral. Mrs. Allen walked slowly across the yard. She didn't move with stiffness, like Gram did when her arthritis flared up. Instead, it looked as if Mrs. Allen barely had the energy to set one foot in front of the other.

How could an old lady run a ranch alone? Even with just a few acres, it must be tough, Sam thought.

Too bad. Sam squashed down her sympathy. There was no excuse for neglecting horses. And, in spite of what Mrs. Allen had said, her neighbors would have been glad to help. Practically any rancher in northern Nevada would *give* her feed, if she couldn't afford to pay for it.

"You old troublemakers," came the rusty voice. "Calico, Ginger, Judge."

Mrs. Allen's voice was feeble, but shuffling hooves and low whinnies said the horses heard her. The flashlight beam lit each of them in turn, as if Mrs. Allen were examining them.

"You are looking poorly, and no wonder. You're as old as me. In horse years, Judge, you're even older. You should all be glue by now. I don't know why I keep you around." The old woman disappeared among the crowding horses.

Plenty of people would love to have those horses, Sam thought. How could Mrs. Allen talk of selling them for glue?

"Hey, old beauty," Mrs. Allen said as she patted

one of the paints. "Don't push." The fragile voice didn't sound mean. Could she have been joking with them?

Mrs. Allen took forever bringing hay from the barn into the pen, and the wind snatched some of it away.

Sam prepared to ride home. The horses were fed, and that was all she'd come for.

Mrs. Allen shuffled to the gate. She made it through, then closed it, but not very well. Sam heard the bolt miss its slot. The gate swung open even before the old woman reached her porch.

Sam waited until the door closed, then shook her head. That solved the mystery of the wandering horses. Mrs. Allen hadn't even looked back. Those horses could just stroll through the open gate and go rambling around the range again.

Sam knew what she had to do, but it made her mad. This was like one of those dreams in which you slogged through deep sand, never getting anywhere, until you woke up out of pure frustration.

Even though this was a waking nightmare — complete with a witch, darkness, and wind so fast it stole her breath — she had no choice. She must make sure that bolt was set. If she didn't, her laziness might cost the horses their lives.

This afternoon, the horses had crossed the highway safely. Tomorrow, they might not be so lucky.

Sam rode Ace at a walk. No longer skittish, he

put every hoof right. He detoured around rocks, walking with such ease, he might never have shied from the ghost horse on the hill.

Once she reached the corral, Sam dismounted and dropped her reins. Ace stood, ground-tied and quiet.

"What a pal," Sam whispered, rubbing his neck.

She hesitated at the gate, looking toward the barn. If Mrs. Allen had used a flashlight, there probably wasn't a light switch just inside the barn door.

It was probably full of rats and insects, too. Sam really didn't feel like blundering around in the dark.

She considered the three horses again. The bay flicked his ears in her direction, but his old teeth kept grinding. That hay would fill their stomachs for now.

Sam secured the latch, but it was still loose. Since it probably wouldn't hold, she got a leather lace from her saddlebags and tied the gate shut.

Just in case one of the horses was clever at escaping, she tied a bowline, then knotted the ends around the two posts.

"That ought to hold them," she muttered to Ace. Then she mounted and started for home.

The lane to Deerpath Ranch seemed shorter on the way out. Soon Ace was loping on a familiar trail across the high desert, but Sam couldn't stop thinking about Mrs. Allen.

Cranky Mrs. Allen had fed her horses, robbing Sam of her chance to be heroic. But they still needed their feet trimmed and a decent enclosure.

She'd tell Gram and Dad. Maybe they'd know who had the authority to keep people from neglecting their horses.

Sam was almost home when she saw headlights coming toward her.

It was Dad. He pulled alongside Ace, and the first thing Sam noticed was that he wasn't wearing his Stetson. Dad's hair was wet and his shirt fresh. He'd probably come in off the range, showered, and planned to relax after dinner. Instead, he was out looking for her.

"You okay?" he asked over the whirring of the truck's engine. "You get lost?"

"I'm fine and I didn't get lost, but . . ." Sam sighed, suddenly feeling the cold on her cheekbones and fingers. "Mrs. Allen isn't taking good care of her stock."

"Did you help her out?"

Sam drew back in surprise. Dad had no use for people who neglected animals. Why was he putting this back on her?

"Not exactly," Sam said.

Dad frowned, but he swung open the truck door.

"Swat Ace on the rump and he'll go home. You can ride back inside where it's warm."

Wind gusted, working its way down Sam's collar. It was too early for snow, but she didn't want to send Ace on alone.

"It's tempting," she said, "but I'll ride him in."

❄ ❄ ❄

Gram had hot chocolate and grilled cheese sandwiches on the kitchen table when Sam came in from the barn. Gram must have cleared away her real dinner hours ago. The sandwiches looked so good, Sam put off showering. It took her about two minutes to wash her hands, sit down, and bite into the golden toast and melted cheese.

She closed her eyes and sighed with satisfaction. When she opened her eyes, Gram and Dad were sitting across from her, looking way too curious.

"The thing is," Sam began, "Mrs. Allen isn't taking care of her horses. I don't know if she can't or just doesn't want to."

"Your dad said you didn't help her." Gram's expression was faintly accusing.

"I couldn't! I wanted to—" Sam stopped because it wasn't really the truth. "She didn't give me a chance. She just yelled at me to get off her property," Sam said. She saw Gram's eyebrows rise. "Really! And her dogs were snarling and jumping at the door. I did leave the jam, though."

"That's good." Gram glanced toward Dad.

"Is she getting around all right?" Dad asked.

Sam pictured Mrs. Allen as she'd moved from the house to the corral. "She's moving slow, but not limping or anything."

"Do you suppose something's wrong?" Gram asked Dad. "I admit I haven't been a very good friend to Trudy since she sold off the ranch."

That didn't sound like Gram. In fact, it didn't even make sense.

When Gram blushed, Sam realized she'd been staring, trying to learn the answer from Gram's face.

"We haven't really been friends since high school," Gram said. "She was a little older, and more interested in art than her neighbors." Gram shrugged. "Her children moved away and then her husband died. I never really knew why she sold off her land."

"Did she have to?" Sam knew many traded the rough ranching life for the security of city jobs, but Mrs. Allen was still here. "Or did she just not want the bother of raising cattle?"

Gram shrugged, and a queasy feeling squirmed through Sam's stomach. "Who bought her ranch?"

"That's no one's business except hers," Dad said, but when his jaw hardened and his eyelids sank a little lower, Sam was afraid she knew the answer.

"Linc Slocum?" she asked. She sipped her cocoa, trying to look like she wasn't prying.

"Could be," Gram said. "I know he paid top dollar for several ranches around here."

Sam's mind was spinning. The property didn't adjoin Slocum's Gold Dust Ranch, so who knew what he'd choose to do with the rest of Deerpath Ranch if it was his.

"How did her ranch look?" Gram asked.

"It was a mess. Fences were down or sagging. The bolt on the corral gate didn't work. There were tumble-weeds piled up against the barn and in the corners of the fences."

"Sounds like she could use some help." Dad pushed his chair back from the table and stood. "How much homework do you have tonight?"

Dad rarely shifted topics so quickly. He really was obsessed with that rotten grade in algebra.

"Dad, what about Mrs. Allen's horses?" she asked.

"Leave that to us," he said. "Homework?"

"I need to take a shower first," Sam protested. "I'm still sort of cold from sitting out on that ridge." She shivered, but Dad's face showed no pity.

"What kind of homework do you have, Samantha?" Gram said.

"I have algebra." Sam moaned. She drained the last swallow of chocolate from her cup as if it could strengthen her. "I always have algebra."

"Better get after it," Dad said. Then, as if it weren't bad enough that she had algebra and Mrs. Allen crowding her mind, he added, "But first, you have a sinkful of dishes to wash. That'll warm you up."

Sam hated it when Gram and Dad ganged up on her, but as soon as she plunged her hands into the mounds of white suds, an exciting idea possessed her brain.

The Phantom had been on that hillside.

Watchful and wary, he'd kept his distance. But he'd left his hidden valley to see her.

If she closed her eyes just until her eyelashes touched, Sam could imagine the soap bubbles were a sculpture of the mustang. She missed him so much.

She swished her hands in the warm water, making the bubbles gallop. And then, Sam's eyes popped open.

She knew where to find him. If she made herself available, the stallion might come to her again.

If that hadn't meant returning to Deerpath Ranch and risking an encounter with Mrs. Allen, she might have tried it that very minute.

"You fall asleep in there?" Dad shouted from the living room.

"No, Dad!" Sam shouted, then sloshed the dishwater loudly. *Some people are never happy*, she thought, but then she smiled.

There must be a way to sneak back onto that ramshackle ranch. She'd find a way to do it tomorrow.

Chapter Four ∾

As THEY CAME DOWN the school bus steps after school the next day, Jen nudged Sam with her elbow.

"Whose truck is that?" Jen asked.

Sam didn't know, but the bus had already driven away, stranding them, when the door to the old, tangerine-colored truck opened.

"Which of you girls is Samantha Forster?"

A woman climbed out. Her hair was dyed jet-black and pulled back in a low ponytail to show big, round silver earrings. They looked like the conchos that decorated the fancy headstall Gram used when she rode Sweetheart.

The woman looked about seventy years old. Her brown eyes were lively, but her face sagged from the corners of her eyes to the corners of her mouth like melted candle wax.

Still, Sam might not have recognized Mrs. Allen if two black-and-white dogs hadn't started bobbing up and down in the front seat, barking and shaking the truck. For a minute, Sam wondered if it was possible the dogs had shrunk.

"Speak up!" the old lady demanded. "Which of you is the Forster girl?"

Jen held Sam's arm, but she stayed quiet, refusing to give her friend away. Still, Sam knew that if Mrs. Allen had even a sketchy memory of her, she wouldn't mistake Jen's long blond braids for her bright auburn hair.

"I am, ma'am." Sam hoped her good manners would soften Mrs. Allen's anger.

"Do you realize that a *social worker* from the county came out to see me today?" Mrs. Allen snarled.

Sam only knew social workers helped people with problems.

"She came out to see if I needed assistance." Mrs. Allen moved closer. "It's not bad enough folks have been holding their breaths since I sold off my land, just waiting for me to kick the bucket. I'm not ready to do that, you can bet, but there was the social worker. And she said *someone* indicated my residence was in disrepair and my animals were neglected."

Sam had already explained everything to Jen, and her friend tried to help.

"Sam was worried about those horses," Jen said.

Mrs. Allen stood in front of them now. Sam was surprised to see she and the old woman were nearly the same height.

"Worried, is she? Well, she won't have to worry about them anymore." Mrs. Allen's tone was threatening.

"You didn't have them put down!" Sam couldn't control the words spurting from between her lips.

"No." Mrs. Allen's voice stayed level. "Since the social worker explained neighbors were worried about me, I said I'd accept the help of some local teenagers."

Sam felt as if the ground had tipped beneath her feet. She knew what was coming and she couldn't help but touch her own breastbone.

"That's right, missy," Mrs. Allen snapped. "You're helping me."

"But why?"

"Did I neglect to mention that your grandmother, that meddling Grace, was over pounding on my door, too?" Mrs. Allen gave Sam a pointed look. "I wouldn't let her in, either, so when the social worker showed up around lunchtime, I knew your pushy family wouldn't be satisfied until . . ." Mrs. Allen's voice trailed off and she suddenly looked exhausted.

"You said teenager*s*," Sam said. Jen stiffened beside her.

"Grace is sending some boy with a broken leg to oversee your work." Mrs. Allen looked dubious.

"Jake," Sam said on a sigh. Though she didn't like the idea of Jake's playing foreman, she'd welcome his company.

"Are you that lazy that you need someone to tell you what to do?" Mrs. Allen asked.

Sam's hands perched on her hips.

If Mrs. Allen knew what needed doing, why didn't she do it herself? Saying that would have been rude, so she didn't. If Gram was already loaning her out to the neighbors, who knew what she might do next.

And Sam knew she'd have little luck complaining to Dad. He always went along with Gram.

"When do I start?" Sam asked. The prospect of more chores made her weary. She had so much homework tonight, she'd already decided she'd have to cut her time with Ace short.

"Tomorrow," Mrs. Allen said. "Bring work gloves." She began walking toward her truck without a please, a thank-you, or even a good-bye.

Jen's voice was thoughtful as she watched Mrs. Allen climb into the driver's seat. "Is there something wrong with her? I mean, is she sick?"

Before Sam could answer, Mrs. Allen pulled up beside them.

Sam waited, watching Mrs. Allen, though the woman looked straight ahead out the windshield as she spoke.

"Thanks for tying the gate closed so the horses didn't get out." Mrs. Allen's jaw was so tight, her words sounded choppy.

"You're welcome."

"I don't thank you for myself, but for the horses," she said. And then she drove away.

When Sam reached home, Gram was nowhere in sight. Dinner was cooking in the Crock-Pot, instead of on the stove. Sam's cookies sat on a paper napkin instead of a plate.

Sam was easing her backpack off one shoulder when steps sounded on the stairs.

"Here you are, at last." Gram bustled into the kitchen, carrying her car keys. "There's something you need to do before starting your homework."

Resentment tightened Sam's muscles. Gram must be talking about Mrs. Allen. "I thought I started tomorrow!" she snapped.

Gram paused and smiled. "Oh, did you talk to Trudy?" Gram held up a finger, as if they could discuss *that* in a minute. "I mean something else. Brynna called and she could use your help—"

Sam couldn't contain a squawk of frustration.

"Samantha!" Gram sounded amazed.

"How would you like it if someone arranged your life without asking you first? I know I'm a kid, but doesn't anyone care what I want? It's not fair to just loan me out to Mrs. Allen, then haul me over to BLM because Dad's *girlfriend* needs me to do something."

Gram slipped into a chair at the kitchen table and sat speechless. As Gram fiddled with her car keys, Sam wondered if she was searching for words or trying to contain her anger.

Sam's irritation melted as Gram studied her. "I'm sorry," she said.

"You're about half right, honey, but that doesn't excuse your rudeness."

"I really am sorry," Sam repeated.

"Maybe I should have checked with you first, but you've always liked helping with horses. Is it different this time?"

"No!" Sam almost shouted. "It's not different."

How silly could she be? She'd been wondering how to get back to Deerpath Ranch and the Phantom. But when Gram had handed her an opportunity, she'd pouted.

"It'll be hard work at Trudy's place, but you were concerned about her wandering horses. This way you'll see that they're cared for."

Sam nodded vigorously.

"And Brynna, you see, is going back to Washington, D.C.," Gram continued.

A tide of mixed feelings rushed over Sam. She'd liked Brynna and respected her, until the BLM woman started dating Dad. Now, she didn't know what to feel.

"She'll be away for two weeks," Gram said. "And before she goes, she wants your help tying up some loose ends."

"What kind of loose ends?"

"She has a number of horses that are considered unadoptable," Gram said.

She walked toward the front door and Sam followed. Sam really could not resist helping horses.

"They probably wouldn't let them run free again," Sam mused.

"Since the drought and then the flood, I can't imagine they would," Gram said as they climbed into her boatlike Buick. "The range is in such poor condition, they wouldn't overburden it with more animals."

"Unadoptable," Sam repeated as Gram aimed her car toward River Bend's bridge. "So, what do you think would happen to them?"

"Well, dear"—Gram's voice was gentle—"in the old days, they used to shoot them."

Sam had never ridden with Gram to BLM's wild horse corrals at Willow Springs. The experience made her appreciate Jake. Even though he'd had his driver's license for only a few months, his driving seemed smoother than Gram's.

"Don't you just hate this road?" Gram said. "You can just about miss the worst bumps, though." Gram swooped from side to side on a surface that felt like rock-hard corduroy.

"Uh-huh," Sam answered. At least the Buick's slow pace kept her teeth from hammering together.

At Thread the Needle, the road became a narrow strip with cliffs plummeting down on each side. Gram slowed even more.

Sam looked to the left and down the steep hillside.

Once, she'd ridden Ace over that maze of antelope trails with the Phantom galloping alongside.

Sam swallowed against the knot of tears in her throat. She missed the stallion so much.

"La Charla doesn't look like much this time of year, does it?" Gram veered toward the edge as she looked down at the river. "No more than a snail trail."

Sam nodded, hoping Gram wouldn't turn to see why she was so quiet.

At last the road started down, and the many corrals of Willow Springs came into view. A few new horses, probably brought in during the flood, shied and ran as a herd when Gram's Buick rolled down the road and parked near the white trucks outside BLM's office.

Sam couldn't wait to get out of the car. Even before she got the door open, she saw Brynna Olson.

Dressed in her khaki uniform, with a reddish braid swaying from side to side behind her shoulders, Brynna Olson marched toward the car.

There was a lot to like about Brynna, Sam thought grudgingly. She was smart, efficient, and she cared more about mustangs than any other adult Sam knew. Still . . .

Sam remembered the first day they'd come up here. Her first reaction had been anger, because she thought Brynna was flirting with Dad. Next, she'd tried to convince herself Brynna had really only been trying to tease Dad into adopting a mustang. And she'd thought Dad had smiled back because it was such a great joke.

Now, Sam knew better.

The two of them hadn't been joking. They'd liked each other right away. In fact, if Sam believed in such things, she might have to admit it had been love at first sight.

Chapter Five ❧

SAM CLIMBED OUT of Gram's Buick and slammed the door harder than necessary. She crossed her arms and stared across the parking area at the corrals of captive mustangs.

She wanted to ignore Brynna Olson's cheery arrival, but the woman's freckled face actually brightened when she saw them.

"Sam, Grace, good to see you."

Gram gave Brynna a quick hug, and Sam's spirits sank lower. *A hug*. Things were worse than she thought, but at least Brynna didn't try it with her. Just in case, Sam took a step back.

Brynna's smile vanished. Her face clouded with confusion.

"Sam"—Brynna's tone turned clipped and formal—"I want you to look at some horses for me."

"The unadoptables. Gram told me. Will they be destroyed?"

"BLM doesn't destroy healthy horses," Brynna said. "But I'm worried about this bunch."

The wind kicked up a whirlwind of dust. Brynna detoured around it. So did Gram and Sam.

Brynna stopped outside a corral shaded by a wall of stacked hay bales. About a dozen horses stood inside the pen.

Gram took an audible breath and let it go. "They're not much to look at. I can't say I'd pay good money for any of them."

Sam leaned against the corral fence and studied the horses a minute longer. She hated to admit it, but most people would agree with Gram.

The horses didn't look like mustangs. Glossy and well-fed, maybe too well-fed, they looked bored and undisturbed by the humans at the fence.

The group was made up of one black, three paints, and assorted bays and sorrels.

"The most outstanding things about them are their ages and lousy conformation," Brynna said.

Sam didn't want to agree, but Brynna was right.

One bay mare had a ewe neck that looked too weak to support her head. A tall bay's showy white socks only emphasized his sickle-hocked hind legs. The black's ears stayed pinned against his neck as if he were permanently cranky, and the scars on his hind legs said he'd kicked—or been kicked—plenty. The smallest of the paints had bumps from withers to tail, as if he'd been stung by a hive of bees. The largest of the paints had a huge belly, leaving no doubt about who got to the feed first.

Sam tried to pick one horse she'd want for her own. It wasn't easy.

The liver chestnut looked pretty good. He strutted like a stallion, and the other horses gave him room, but his extreme Roman nose gave him the face of a fierce dinosaur.

Wait. Sam moved a little farther down the fence. What about that sorrel? Ears pricked and eyes wide, she was a pretty little animal whose flaxen mane streamed over her cinnamon shoulders like honey.

"She's beautiful," Sam said. "I can't believe no one would adopt her."

As Sam pointed her out, the filly trotted toward the fence.

All at once, Sam ached with pity. The filly's knees were aimed to the sides instead of straight ahead. Her gait was so wobbly, Sam feared she'd fall.

"She's young," Brynna said. "Those legs might straighten out, or they could be corrected by surgery. She is a beauty. Plus, she's curious and eager to learn." Brynna paused and shook her head. "But no one's willing to take a chance on her."

"Did they all come from around here?" Gram asked.

"No. They're from all over the place — Oregon, California, some from down near Las Vegas. Only one of the paints could be called local." Brynna gestured south. "The big one came in with a bunch from the Smoke Creek desert."

Though her voice was all business, Brynna wiggled her fingers toward the sorrel filly, tempting her a few steps closer. "These horses have been moved from one adoption center to another," she continued.

"And that's why they're so tame?" Sam interrupted.

Brynna nodded. "They've been loaded and unloaded, herded, and fed by humans. Some have been captive for over a year. When they leave here next week, they'll go to a big pasture in the Midwest where they'll stay for life."

"That doesn't sound so bad," Gram said. "Though I'm not sure I like the fact that my tax dollars will be supporting a retirement home for horses."

"Lots of folks feel that way," Brynna admitted.

As the two women discussed money, Sam wished she could turn these horses loose and watch them run free. They'd look like different animals. But they'd probably never gallop across the range again. These mustangs would graze away their lives, placid as dairy cows.

Sam turned around in time to see Brynna fall silent. Words seemed to jam in her throat as she glanced back toward her office. "I'm leaving for two weeks of meetings in Washington, D.C. Norman White is taking my place. He's"—Brynna seemed to be biting her tongue to stay professional—"not a horseman," she managed. "And I'm not sure what decisions might be made while I'm gone."

Sam watched Brynna shift, then swallow hard. Why was the woman so uneasy?

Sam sorted through all Brynna had said today, until her mind clicked on a single phrase.

BLM doesn't destroy healthy horses.

Was Brynna worried that Norman White wouldn't certify these mustangs as healthy?

But Brynna's and Gram's conversation had supplied the reason. Money.

Norman White might try to save the government money by having old or ill-formed horses put down.

Not only would that be cruel, it would be unfair. These horses were wild animals. They hadn't been bred to measure up to human standards.

"How can I help?" Sam asked.

"Do you know anyone who'd want them?" Brynna didn't sound very hopeful.

"That's it?" Sam asked. Surely, Brynna could come up with something better than that. "Didn't you ask me up here to help with some plan?"

Brynna shook her head, looking forlorn.

"I've run out of plans and time," she said.

Sam did her best to consider the horses all over again.

If she were a millionaire, she'd adopt them, put them in a huge pasture, and hope their wild natures returned. But she knew only one millionaire, and he'd never help. All Linc Slocum's possessions were beautiful or valuable. These horses were neither.

Who, then? Jake's Three Ponies Ranch couldn't afford twelve useless horses. Jen's family had already been forced to sell their land and stock to Slocum. Sam couldn't think of anyone with both a soft heart and money.

"What about the HARP program?" Sam said suddenly. "These horses would be perfect. The little sorrel is half tame already. And kids would like those pintos."

"I already tried HARP," Brynna said. "Their funding is looking shaky. They won't take on more horses or kids until it's a sure thing."

Sam stared at the captive mustangs until they blurred. Who would want a dozen horses, mostly old and ugly?

Sam rubbed her eyes. "Dust from that whirlwind," she muttered to Gram and Brynna. But Sam was thinking, *They don't deserve to die.*

The next morning, as Sam turned a corner and started down the hall to her locker at Darton High, she saw Jake. He looked angry, and she'd bet it had something to do with being loaned out to Mrs. Allen.

She could be wrong. Since his accident, Jake had been quarrelsome. He'd argue over anything.

In fact, Jake was fighting his broken leg as if it were a living, breathing enemy.

And he was winning.

Sam hid her smile. Not many guys would be clumping around in a walking cast, without a crutch, long before his predicted recovery.

The effort cost Jake a lot. His black hair didn't look like a warrior's this morning. Locks of it had straggled loose from the leather tie. The blue tee-shirt he wore over jeans looked rumpled. And he wore tennis shoes because the cast wouldn't allow him to wear boots.

If there was one thing Jake hated worse than wearing tennis shoes, it was sympathy. If she pampered him, he'd be even madder. So she didn't.

When he shifted to face her, frown lines marked his forehead and Sam knew she'd catch the blame.

"It's not my fault." Sam dialed her locker combination.

"Right," Jake snarled.

"Okay," she allowed, "in a little tiny way, it is. But you wouldn't have let those horses wander around hungry."

"Bet me," Jake said.

"You would not." Sam dismissed his sarcasm by rolling her eyes toward the ceiling. She held her books against one hip and slammed her locker door. "Besides, it'll do you good to work. You've been so cranky since you haven't been able to ride, no one can stand to be around you."

Sam pressed her lips together. That had been a little harsh.

"So?" Jake's expression didn't change, but he

glanced over one shoulder. He'd never admit it, but he was relieved to see his friends nearby. One, a hard case named Darrell, gave Jake a slit-eyed nod of reassurance.

"Besides, you've always liked bossing me around."

"It's not that," Jake muttered. "I'd just rather work for your dad or school Teddy Bear."

Teddy Bear was the curly Bashkir that Jake had been riding on the stormy day he'd broken his leg. When the gelding had fallen, he'd pinned Jake's leg against a riverbank that had been as hard as concrete.

"Dad said Mr. Martinez is amazed by the progress you made with Teddy Bear," Sam said, watching Jake carefully. She could tell he was still sad that Mr. Martinez had trailered the horse home. "And Dad said you both made an extra hundred dollars because Mr. Martinez was so pleased. How can you complain?"

Jake gave a gruff sound that said Sam knew how. And she did. She wouldn't trade her riding time for any amount of money.

Sam would have felt sorrier for Jake if goofy Darrell hadn't been eavesdropping with a smirk.

"So, what exactly are we supposed to do?" Jake asked. He glanced over his shoulder to see what Sam was watching. Of course, Darrell played innocent.

"I don't know." Sam moved toward her first class, but Jake just stood there, making her look cruel for deserting him, so she stopped.

"The place is a mess," she said. "Everything needs paint, and she's got about fifty miles of fence falling down."

Jake groaned, but Sam had expected that. All cowboys hated mending fence.

"I'm not looking forward to it much myself," Sam said. But then she saw Jake wasn't groaning about the fence, he was checking out Jen.

Dressed in retina-searing yellow jeans, black high-top sneakers, a black shirt, and her dark-framed glasses, Jen sauntered toward them with braids swinging. She wore a wicked grin at Jake's discomfort. Jen and Jake didn't like each other any more than Darrell and Sam did.

"Jake!" Sam snapped her fingers to recapture his attention. "We've got to do it. If fixing that fence keeps one horse from getting hit on the highway—"

"Stop! Oh, please stop!" Darrell lurched into the conversation. As the first bell rang, he clasped his hands against his chest. "You're breaking my heart."

Sam really couldn't stand the kid. There were some things you didn't joke about. Like hungry horses.

"Darrell, you are such a—"

"C'mon, Sam." Jen gave Sam a push toward history class.

They detoured around Rachel Slocum. Darton High's princess wore a black leather skirt that barely allowed her to walk, but she apparently had enough breath to block traffic with her body while sweet-talking with her boyfriend, Kris Cameron.

He was absolutely the cutest guy at Darton High, and if his infatuation with Rachel hadn't said bad things about his IQ, Sam would have thought he was perfect. In fact, his broad shoulders and quarterback mystique almost made up for his lack of judgment over girls.

Blinking to break her gaze, Sam looked back to see if Jake was still there. He was.

"You owe me one," he shouted after her.

"In your dreams!" Sam yelled.

"That's exactly what I wanted to talk with you about."

Sam jumped at Mrs. Ely's voice. Her history teacher stood in the classroom doorway, and even though she was also Jake's mother, she didn't reprimand Sam for shouting after him. Sam guessed Mrs. Ely knew her son could be annoying.

"You want to talk about my dreams?" Sam asked.

"Dreams, fame, and fortune—you name it," Mrs. Ely said. "We've got a minute before the bell. Why don't you step into my office."

Sam followed Mrs. Ely across the classroom, into the tiny office beyond.

There, Mrs. Ely handed her a sealed brown envelope.

"Here's the entry blank for the Night Magic contest."

Sam nodded. For months, Mrs. Ely and Mr. Blair, Sam's journalism teacher, had been encouraging her to enter the photography contest.

Sam had taken a great picture of an escaped stallion rearing against the moon. But it had been published on the front page of the local paper. Publication made it ineligible for the contest.

"The deadline is coming up, so think of something," Mrs. Ely urged. "If Wyatt or Grace gives you a hard time about being out after dark, tell them to call me. I'd offer to send my son along, but—" Mrs. Ely broke off.

Her eyes studied her office door. Not quite closed, it moved a fraction of an inch. As Mrs. Ely leaned forward to swing it open, Sam spotted black leather.

Chapter Six ᔢ

"ℛACHEL?" Mrs. Ely asked.

Trust Rachel to look totally relaxed, even though anyone would guess she'd been eavesdropping.

"Mrs. Ely, I was just wondering if that homework on ancient Eygpt is due today?" Rachel frowned so sincerely, a tiny little wrinkle appeared between her brows.

Sam didn't buy it. Judging by Mrs. Ely's tone, neither did she. "Yes, of course, Rachel."

"All right. Just making sure." Rachel nodded. Then, as a bell shrilled through the school, marking the beginning of first period, Rachel gave Sam a sisterly look that said they should both be in their seats.

Sam held up the envelope, in a sort of promise to Mrs. Ely. "Thanks."

Rachel noticed the movement, lingered, and clearly hoped Sam would say what was in the envelope. Sam just walked to her seat, thinking that if there was a nosier girl at Darton High, she didn't want to meet her.

Rachel's snooping didn't make sense. Why should she be interested in the lives of others, when her own was like a fairy tale? She had money for every whim. She traveled all over the world. Her mother had a horse farm in England and her father owned a ranch with more luxuries than a resort. Whose life could possibly be more interesting than Rachel's?

Sam pushed those thoughts aside and took notes while Mrs. Ely lectured. Careful not to let the teacher notice, Sam slipped the contest brochure out of the envelope and then under her notebook paper, so she could sneak peeks at it.

Night Magic was a contest that encouraged amateur photographers to test their skills in low light.

Staring at the brochure, she remembered a time she'd seen the Phantom and his mares in the moonlight. Their beauty had filled her with wonder, but did she want to share the dreamy vision?

Sam glanced up. From across the room, Rachel was watching her. Sam shot her a bored look, but she wondered why Rachel—a junior taking a freshman class—wasn't paying attention to the teacher. She'd probably flunked world history the first time, and Mrs. Ely wouldn't pass her based on popularity or her daddy's clout.

Just then, Sam met Mrs. Ely's eyes.

Oh, shoot. Mrs. Ely wouldn't cut her any slack just because she liked her, either. Sam shoved the brochure completely under her notes.

She'd gotten pretty interested in Mrs. Ely's lecture about Isis and King Tut and mummification when thoughts of Deerpath Ranch and the Phantom plopped right back into the middle of her imagination.

Just over the hill from the ranch, past a series of roller-coaster canyons and gullies, lay the desert. In her mind's eye, Sam saw the alkali flats spread with moonlight and wild horses.

If she could make the picture materialize, it would be a winner. And it was just barely possible the prize money would be enough to save the unadoptable wild horses.

After school, Sam and Jen burst from the building with hundreds of other students. At the sight of her dad's truck in Darton High's parking lot, Sam stopped so suddenly that other students rushing homeward slammed into her.

"Sorry," Sam said as the kids cut around her, but she was nervous.

What was wrong? Even when she was a kid, she'd ridden the bus home. Dad had never picked her up from school.

"Is that your dad?" Jen asked.

"Yeah."

"Did you know he was coming?"

"No. I wonder what he wants." Sam thought she sounded properly casual. "You want to come?"

"No way," Jen said. "In my experience, when parents do something weird, it usually means trouble."

"I've been good," Sam said.

Jen's arm swung around Sam's shoulder in a hug, and then she whispered, "Don't look now, but you are *not* the only source of trouble in this world, or even in your family."

"True." Sam gave her friend a lopsided smile. "See ya later."

"Call me!" Jen jogged toward the bus.

"I will." Sam waved, sighed, walked over to her dad's truck, and opened the truck door. "What's wrong?"

Sam scooted inside, fastened her seat belt, and noticed the Stetson sitting on the tattered upholstery between them. Then she saw Dad's smile.

"Nothing's wrong. Can't I pick up my own daughter from school?"

"Yeah, but . . . you don't. Ever. What are you doing here?"

"I had a dentist appointment." Dad laughed as he pulled out of the parking lot and into traffic.

"Oh, that's all right, then." Still, Sam watched him from the corner of her eye.

"I got you some work gloves, too. Yours are fine for riding, but the kind of work you'll be doing over at Trudy Allen's might get you cut up."

If Dad thought the work she was going to be doing was hard, it really would be.

"Thanks," she said. "I'm worried about Dark Sunshine, though, Dad. When am I going to exercise her? What if I lose all the ground I've gained with her?"

"We'll work that out."

Sam tried to read Dad's tone. Though he was a kind man, he didn't have much use for mustangs. Especially now, during drought times, he grumbled that they consumed food and water needed for cattle.

Even though Dark Sunshine was their responsibility now, as part of the HARP program, Sam knew he'd see gentling the mare as secondary to helping a neighbor.

But he didn't say so. Instead, Dad asked, "Want to stop at Clara's before going over to Mrs. Allen's?"

Sam couldn't think of the diner in Alkali without feeling her mouth water. Clara served CD-size hamburgers, crispy fries, and the best chocolate upside-down cake in the world—a sign on the diner's wall even said so.

But she tried to be mature, instead of drooling.

"Do we have time?" she asked with her fingers crossed.

"I sent Ross and Pepper over to haul out the worst of the tumbleweeds," Dad said. "So you've got a head start."

It was just like cowboys to leave the fence for her and Jake, Sam thought, but she was grateful.

"Then, sure. I'd love to stop at Clara's."

Wind buffeted the truck as they rode in silence. Sam didn't mind. She stared out the passenger window, feeling content. She knew each mile of the trip from Darton to River Bend Ranch. Sand-colored hills rolled away from the road. Cottonwood trees showed green against them, marking the paths of streams running down from the Calico Mountains.

Anything could blend into that wild country and vanish. Gram had said, once, that Sam's mother's greatest fear had been that her curious daughter would become lost on the range before she was old enough to take care of herself.

When Sam had been a toddler, someone—it could have been Dad, Gram, or her mother; she couldn't remember just who—had told her the only way she'd earn a spanking would be by leaving the ranch grounds.

Now, Sam kind of understood why they'd wanted to keep her so close. Even in good weather, a small child would be difficult to find out there. If a snow-storm blew in, she'd have been lost for good.

Sam shivered. This year, she'd ridden into those hills plenty of times, chasing wild horses. She'd always come back alive. She hoped her mother could look down and know little Samantha had grown up enough to take care of herself.

Gravel crunched under the truck's tires, startling Sam from her thoughts, as they pulled into the diner's gravel parking lot. Inside, they split a hamburger and fries.

"Don't want to spoil our dinner," Dad said.

"Especially after the other night." Sam grimaced at the memory of waiting on Mrs. Allen's hillside while Gram wondered where she was, then made a special dinner for her.

"She understood." Dad used a fry to dot up a few grains of salt, then set it aside without taking a bite. "I think you ought to know something about Brynna."

Here it comes. Sam's hands closed into fists and her shoulders tensed. She choked on the bite she'd been chewing. Coughing, she took a sip of her soda, and finally swallowed.

"It's not that serious," Dad said.

Why the heck was he smiling? What if he announced he and Brynna were engaged?

Why couldn't adults go steady? There must be a step between dating and engagement. Anything would be better than that, she thought.

Unless they'd eloped.

Sam shot a quick look at Dad's left hand. It was brown, scarred from hard work, but beautifully bare of rings.

"I thought you should know why she has to go to Washington this week. Go ahead and finish." Dad nodded at the suddenly abandoned hamburger.

Sam ate, chewing automatically. She swallowed.

"Is it about the mustangs?"

"Yeah." Dad folded his fingers together. "Some boss way on up the line heard Brynna'd gotten friendly with 'the locals.' They're worried she might be abusing her position to . . . uh, please 'em."

Sam parted her lips, then closed them. Brynna was always professional. She did what she knew was right, no matter whose feelings she hurt.

"The locals," Sam repeated. "Does that mean you or me?"

"Don't think we'll know till she gets back there. Seems to me it must be you. She's made lots of cattle ranchers miserable."

"What do they think she's done for me?"

"Some would say she shouldn't have turned out that gray stud once he'd been caught."

"But he was trapped by Flick, a rustler. The Phantom wasn't taken in a gather—"

"Still," Dad said.

"Do you know anything about the man who's taking her place? Norman somebody?"

"She told me what she told you and Gram."

"C'mon, Dad. I bet she told you something else."

"Not a thing," he answered, and that was that. "We better get going." He stood and fished his wallet from his pocket.

"I'm no slacker, Dad," Sam said as they walked

back to the truck. "But I wish I didn't have to go work for Mrs. Allen."

"Why's that? You'd be working at home. Afraid Jake's going to boss you around?"

"Like that's something new," Sam grumbled.

"You can't still be afraid of those dogs."

Sam took a deep breath. "I'm never afraid of dogs, you know that. But when I was over there, they were flinging themselves against the door like they wouldn't mind taking a bite out of me."

"Honey, those two dogs are Boston bulls. They're no bigger than chickens."

Sam giggled.

"They're named Imp and Angel," Dad added. "Just in case you need to call 'em off."

Ace was neighing when Sam arrived at River Bend Ranch. Dad delivered her to the front door at about the same time she would have arrived if she'd ridden the bus and walked home.

Feeling too full and cozy for labor, she pulled on work clothes just the same. By the time she buttoned up a flannel overshirt, she'd remembered she didn't mind working with Jake.

When it was just the two of them, he was her friend. Besides, it was a beautiful lope over to Deerpath Ranch and Ace was ready to go. She couldn't help thinking how happy Mrs. Allen's horses would be for the company.

Maybe, just maybe, the Phantom would come down from the Calico Mountains. She'd think about that, not mean Mrs. Allen and her spear-studded fence.

Chapter Seven ❧

CALICO, GINGER, AND Judge stood neighing at the fence when Sam rode up on Ace. For the last half mile, coming up the lane, Ace had acted feisty, pulling at the bit, slewing from side to side as if he wanted to gallop. Sam didn't let him, but she was glad the little horse was having fun.

Jake had beaten her to Deerpath Ranch, and he wasn't alone. Two of his brothers—from here it looked like Nate and maybe Brian—were working together like a machine on one length of fence while Jake waited for her.

"About time you got here," he grumbled.

Sam dismounted and led Ace to the corral. "I wonder what I'd do," she said, trying to sound miserable, "if just once you acted glad to see me."

Jake's half grin said he didn't feel guilty. "I just saw you at school."

"I know." As Sam opened the corral, she noticed

someone had fixed the latch.

"If you want to get your feelings hurt," Jake went on, "pout because Nate and Brian have already reset a dozen posts. All we have to do is tighten wire, but they have such a head start, we'll never catch 'em." Jake squinted into the late-afternoon sun, watching his brothers dig, then fill. "And they're going to rub it in."

"I'm hurrying." Sam pulled Ace's bridle from his head while the other horses nudged him with eager muzzles. "Look how well Ace gets along with Mrs. Allen's horses. Why is he the outcast at home and the most popular guy over here?" Sam gave the bay a last pat.

In addition to the government freeze brand on his neck, Ace wore other scars. His gleaming rump had been raked by Strawberry's teeth and pounded by Tank's hooves. Only Gram's mare, Sweetheart, was pleased to share a pen with Ace.

"Jake, really, why do they like him better?"

"The horse psychologist is closed," Jake said. He shoved a tool belt at Sam. "I can already hear the jokes about the gimp and the girl."

"You're imagining things," Sam said as she strapped the tool belt around her waist. One loop held a hammer, and a leather pocket was filled with metal staples.

While daylight lasted, she and Jake moved along the fence line. He used a fence tool to pull the wire creaking tight. Then, hands snug inside her new gloves, Sam hammered in metal staples to hold the wire in place.

After a half hour of this, Sam paused. In spite of the cold wind, sweat dripped from her brow. She looked toward the brooding Victorian house. She could see Mrs. Allen's tangerine-colored truck in the driveway, so she must be home.

"Has she come out of the house since you've been here?"

"No." Jake shrugged. "Why should she?"

"It'd be nice, that's all. She could bring us lemonade or something."

Jake gave a grunting laugh. "I don't think she's the lemonade type."

It was getting dark and hard to see when Sam accidentally hit her thumb with the hammer.

"Ow!" It started throbbing right away, and it served her right. She'd been gazing toward the house again.

"That's what you get," Jake mused.

"Why does she need these fences fixed anyway?" Sam dropped her hammer, then tucked her injured thumb under her arm. "She sold all her cattle."

Taking the weight off his injured leg, Jake leaned against a post weathered gray by years of sun and snow, and shook his head. "'Cause that's the way it should be, Samantha. You don't want posts leaning and wire down where someone could come galloping along and trip on it." He sighted down the fence line and checked to see that it was straight. "You just don't."

On the third day, the work was nearly done, and still Mrs. Allen hadn't come out of her house to say thanks.

There'd been no sign of the Phantom, either. All Sam knew was that she was getting behind in her classes, she hadn't had a single hour to ride with Jen, and she was no closer to taking the Night Magic pictures than she'd been three days ago.

Sam's frustration grew. Finally, she dropped her hammer back through the leather loop at her waist and turned toward Jake with her hands on her hips.

"I'm going to go ask her for a drink."

"We have a water jug in the truck," Jake told her, but he looked amused, as if he knew this march on Mrs. Allen's house wasn't about thirst.

"Thanks, but I'm going up there anyway."

"Just stay put, Brat. Why stir up trouble?"

Sam had given up sticking out her tongue at Jake when he called her Brat. And this time it had actually sounded affectionate, but Sam kept walking.

They were doing the neighborly thing, so why couldn't Mrs. Allen?

"Ten to one you come back empty-handed," Jake called after her. When that didn't make her turn back, he added, "Watch out for those dogs."

Sam ignored the spear-shaped fence posts. As she

lifted the latch on the black iron gate, she waited for the sound of the yapping dogs.

Nothing.

The scent of roses, dried and sagging on their bushes, came to her. She wanted to leave the gate open for a quick getaway, but years of conditioning wouldn't allow it.

Courtesy said if you came to a gate and it was latched, you passed through, then latched it after you. If you came to a gate that was open, you left it open.

But as she shut the gate behind her, Sam wondered if she was closing off her escape.

The dogs didn't bark when she walked up the porch steps or when she knocked on the door. Though the truck hadn't moved in three days, the house felt empty.

Sam knocked harder on the door and it opened a few inches.

Inside, it was dark. She caught the smell of tea and mentholated rub. No one called "Come in," but Sam wouldn't have gone even if someone had.

"No way," she muttered to herself. She'd seen enough horror movies to know a silent house with an open door was an invitation to disaster.

Sam came back down the steps more slowly. Just as she turned toward the gate, wind rattled some dried hollyhocks and brought the sound of the dogs. They weren't yapping. She heard the click of toenails on a hardwood floor.

"Angel, Imp, quit pacing." The voice was Mrs. Allen's, but it sounded gentler than usual.

Sam followed a concrete path that looped around the side of the house to a separate building. It was round, with windows set high in the walls. In the late-afternoon sun, they turned to flats of gold.

"Hello?" Mrs. Allen called, as if she'd heard Sam's footsteps.

Sam wanted to leave, but Jake's bet that she'd return empty-handed echoed in her mind. Would she ever outgrow the temptation of a dare?

Not today. Sam drew a deep breath. She'd faced Brahma bulls, wild stallions, and a pack of coyotes. She could by golly face an old lady and two yappy dogs.

"Hi, Mrs. Allen. It's Samantha. I just—"

Sam's irritation faded. She wasn't invading a witch's lair. This was a beautiful art studio. She searched for words that would make sense.

"I just wondered if I could get a drink of water," she finally said.

Golden light crowded the studio, hiding nothing. Mrs. Allen sat in front of an easel, brush poised above one of the weirdest paintings Sam had ever seen.

"Of course you may," Mrs. Allen said.

"I didn't know you were an artist," Sam blurted.

Mrs. Allen shrugged. "No reason you would. Northern Nevada isn't the best place to sell the work I do."

Sam could see why. The paintings were of plants, but they weren't normal. They were lush and green with vivid scarlet throats and lips edged with glittering teeth.

"Carnivorous plants," Mrs. Allen said. "Venus flytraps, mainly, although that one"—she pointed across the studio—"is an English sundew."

"They look almost alive."

Mrs. Allen didn't answer, but the little black-and-white dogs sniffed Sam's feet and knees in a friendly way. When Sam reached down to pet their sleek little heads, she got chills. But it wasn't the dogs that troubled her. It was Mrs. Allen.

Why would anyone paint portraits of meat-eating plants?

Maybe she just didn't understand an artist's mind, Sam thought. Then she saw other canvases stacked on the floor in a corner. They were smaller, not much bigger than place mats, and they were painted in an entirely different style.

Where the plants were still and detailed down to the last spiky tooth, these paintings were blurred with movement. It took Sam a minute to see that they were of wild horses. Gray, black, and orange-red, they streaked across featureless white.

"Wild horses on the playa," Sam blurted. This was art she understood.

Mrs. Allen stood, heels striking the wood floor like a slap. The dogs backed away from Sam, eyes fixed on their mistress.

She wiped her brush on her smock.

"There's water over there." The gentleness in Mrs. Allen's voice vanished as she hurried Sam on her way. She pointed at plastic-wrapped cases of bottled water.

Sam grabbed a bottle. It seemed to take forever to work it loose of the plastic. In the meantime, one dog began growling.

"Thanks," Sam said, and hurried from the studio.

Mrs. Allen liked horses. Sam already knew that, and it showed in the paintings. So why had she switched to painting those scary plants?

By the time Sam reached Jake, she'd decided she couldn't figure it out alone. And Jake wasn't in the mood to help.

"I don't care what Gram says," she muttered. "Mrs. Allen is weird."

Jake didn't ask why she said it, just threw his weight against a post and gestured for her to pound in a staple.

As he did, Sam noticed Jake's lips were pressed together so hard, they looked pale in his mahogany face.

"How's your leg?" she asked.

"Fine."

Of course Jake would say that, even if he were faint from pain, so she tried again. "How long until the cast comes off?"

"Look, Brat, do you want to work or gossip? It's Friday night. I have other things to do besides hug fence posts. I was really hoping we could finish up so I wouldn't have to come back out here next week. Nate and Brian have work to do at the ranch."

It *was* a lot of work, and Sam hadn't told anyone about her nose-diving grades in history and algebra. She'd been too tired to do her reading assignments, so of course both teachers had sprung pop quizzes on the class. Plus, she'd blown a small deadline in journalism.

"I was thinking we could get Darrell and Jen to help us finish up," Sam suggested.

"Maybe." Jake didn't sound enthusiastic, but he moved a little faster. "I don't think she's paying us, though. This is just sort of a test of neighborliness."

It was dusk when Jake and his brothers threw their gear into the back of their truck. The truck bounded over the field, and the Ely boys waved at Sam as she walked toward the corral to saddle Ace.

Clumps of yellow cheat grass showed where there had been mounds of tumbleweeds; the corral gate was locked, not creaking in the wind; and someone had fixed that broken shutter. Things looked a lot better, but was it worth the effort if Mrs. Allen didn't care?

"Hey there, guys," Sam said as the horses greeted her with nickers. At least they were happy with the changes going on around them.

And Sam had to admit Mrs. Allen loved her horses. These three hadn't been starved, after all. They were old and a little gaunt, but she couldn't hold that against their owner.

Sam stretched and felt a tendon complain. Tomorrow was Saturday, and Gram usually gave her an extra hour to cuddle down under her quilt and sleep in. She could hardly wait.

She smoothed the saddle blanket over Ace's back, then slung the saddle up and centered it. A nice ride home, dinner, and maybe she'd watch a movie later and have some popcorn.

Gram might have even planned something as a reward. Just as long as she didn't ask how math was going, Sam thought it might be a good weekend.

"Samantha Forster."

Sam was drawing Ace's cinch tight when Mrs. Allen's voice stopped her.

Mrs. Allen's artist smock was gone. She wore baggy jeans that looked like they might have belonged to her late husband.

"Yes, ma'am," Sam answered, but a voice in her head was chanting, *Please don't ask me to do anything else, please don't ask me, please don't.*

"Tomorrow the farrier is coming. These horses haven't had their feet seen to in some time. And since you were the one who pointed this out, it seems only right you be here to help. Calico, you see, doesn't appreciate the handling of her feet."

Something in Mrs. Allen's eyes convinced Sam the old lady just wanted company. Sam wanted to turn her down, but she wasn't sure she could.

For a few seconds, Sam considered the big paint horses. She was so tired, she couldn't remember which was which. While she tried to decide, an idea sparked and flared in her mind. Something to do with pintos . . . but then it was gone.

"I'd be glad to help," she said, and noticed that lightning didn't really strike liars. "What time is the farrier coming?"

"First thing in the morning," Mrs. Allen said. "I'll see you about seven-thirty."

Sam was riding down the lane toward home when she noticed the tree house.

She drew rein and looked up into the branches, wondering if her eyes were deceiving her in the gray light. No, there were pegs set in the side of the tree. Steps.

It was hard to believe Mrs. Allen had had kids. Jake had said she wasn't the lemonade type, and she didn't seem like the mother type, either. But someone had built this tree house for young explorers, and Sam would bet it gave a great view of the ranch lands, hills, and canyons beyond.

When Sam reached home, Gram was serving a dinner of ham with baked potatoes and mounds of broccoli covered with cheese sauce. And she said a boy named Darrell had called.

"Did he say what he wanted?" Sam asked.

"No. He wouldn't even leave a number."

Sam was mystified. Unless he'd called to apologize for teasing her every time he felt like it—and that seemed unlikely—she couldn't imagine what he'd want. Right now, though, it didn't matter. If it was important, he'd call back.

Sam was so hungry, she ate without talking. It wasn't until she'd cleaned her plate for the second time that she realized Dad was even quieter than usual. Then he left the table without dessert.

"What's up?" Sam asked when she and Gram were alone. "Is he pining because Brynna's gone?"

Sam wanted to take back her catty remark immediately when Gram looked down, folded her napkin in quarters, and shook her head.

"Gracious, I thought Wyatt would talk with you about this, but I see he's left it for me."

"Left what?" Sam didn't like the careful way Gram was talking.

"Well, you've a right to know." Gram met Sam's eyes. "Your Dad talked with Dr. Scott today."

Glen Scott was the levelheaded young vet who'd doctored the Phantom in the rodeo arena, who'd helped set the stallion free. He'd displayed such a connection with wild horses, Brynna had hired him as Willow Springs's on-call veterinarian.

In addition, he'd become a favorite among the

local ranchers for all equine problems.

Sam knew what that meant. Something was wrong with one of the horses. She couldn't bear to ask which one.

"Dr. Scott told Wyatt that those horses up at Willow Springs are in big trouble." Gram had to clear her throat before she could continue, and Sam was still feeling grateful that nothing was wrong with her own horses, when Gram added, "Norman White wants to put them down."

Chapter Eight ❧

$\mathcal{B}$RYNNA HAD ONLY been gone two days. This couldn't be happening.

Sam's dinner sat suddenly heavy in her stomach.

She told herself the substitute director was just bluffing, showing how important he was, so the staff at Willow Springs would respect him.

Dr. Scott wouldn't let him get away with it, and neither would the man Sam called Bale-Tosser. Why did she always forget his name? The big bearded man was Brynna's right hand at Willow Springs, and she'd bet Norman White had decided to show him who was boss.

"What did Dr. Scott say, exactly?" Sam asked.

"He's been notified by Mr. White to stand by to, well, perform euthanasia—"

"Kill them, he means." Sam felt as if someone had clamped her entire body in snow. "No, Gram. We can't let him do it."

"Samantha," Gram said carefully, "you saw those animals. Brynna knew death was a possibility for them when she left. Those horses can't be happy—"

"But, Gram, they shouldn't die just because they're old and not so pretty . . . " Sam's voice trailed off, then her strength flooded back. "Those are not good reasons to kill them."

"I know." Gram rose from the table and began doing the dishes, even though the chore was Sam's.

As the plates swished in soapy water, Sam tried to review the horses in her mind. She couldn't stop thinking about the little sorrel with the weak legs. Brynna thought the filly might heal, but now she might not even get the chance.

Sam bolted up from the table and ran into the living room, where Dad had settled in his recliner with the newspaper.

"Dad, Gram told me what Dr. Scott said." She didn't give her father a chance to speak. "We've got to help those horses. We can't let that man put them down."

"What would you like to do, Sam?" Dad sounded too calm.

Why was he even asking? There was only one solution.

"Adopt them. We have lots of land, and even though they're not useful horses now, Jake and I could work with them." Sam felt a swoop of despair. School, horses, photography, chores . . . she had too much work to take on more. But maybe Dad hadn't noticed.

"Samantha, do you remember Banjo?" Dad asked.

"Of course I do."

Banjo had been Dad's best roping and cutting horse. Yet Dad had sold him after the flood. Dad was hinting at something Sam didn't want to hear.

"If we had spare cash laying around to spend on horses, do you think I'd have sold Banjo?"

Sam shook her head so hard, her bangs covered her eyes. She pushed them back, giving herself an instant to think.

"But BLM wouldn't make us pay the adoption fee, I bet. I mean, they wouldn't earn anything from the horses, but they wouldn't have to pay the vet to put them down, and we could just haul them away . . . "

Dad let Sam's weak words echo around her. When she didn't admit how immature her arguments were, Dad set his jaw, looking angry and disappointed.

"You're listening to your heart and not your head, Sam. We raise cattle and we school horses. They all eat, but they give something back. Money. We can't be buying old mustangs to put on our land for nothing."

"It's not for nothing!"

"I don't like reminding you we've got Buddy, a meat animal we'll never butcher, and that buckskin mare, who's half crazy. She'll probably never be rideable." Dad held up his hand to hush Sam's protest. "Of course it's not her fault, but what are you thinking? I'm a cattleman. I will not buy mustangs and purposely put them on my land to compete with my cattle."

"But, Dad—"

"Samantha, this conversation is not going anywhere you want it to go."

"Dad"—she tried to sound calm—"Brynna told me the horses don't compete with the cattle. They don't run them off from the grass. They just eat right alongside them."

"And how is that better?"

Sam knew he was right. The grass eaten by the mustangs still wouldn't be there for hungry cattle. She tried another approach, even though she knew this battle was lost.

"But, Dad, there's this beautiful little sorrel, and a bunch of big paints. You know, I've heard lots of people are partial to loud-colored horses. I could even have Aunt Sue ask around in San Francisco!"

"Samantha . . ."

"Dad, I don't know why—" Sam broke off. "It would only be for a little while. I could find someone—"

"This conversation is over." Dad's voice trembled with anger.

"I'm sorry, Dad, but—"

"But nothing, young lady. Remember what puts food on your table and feed in Ace's manger."

Usually, Dad stormed from the room when he was angry. This time he didn't.

Sam turned toward the stairs. It wasn't fair. These horses could die because of Dad's stubbornness.

"Did you want to be excused?" Dad asked before Sam could take a step.

"Yes, sir." Sam's fingers were clenched in fists at her sides, but she tried not to let anger color her voice. "May I please be excused?"

"Go ahead."

Two could be stubborn, Sam thought. Dad was probably still sitting downstairs, expecting her to apologize. But if he wouldn't, she wouldn't.

She lay on her bed, staring at the ceiling, her algebra book open next to her.

Her feelings were a tangle. She was amazed Dad hadn't grounded her for arguing. She was angry because he wouldn't save those horses. And she was confident she'd think of a solution.

Determination kept her awake until Dad and Gram went to bed. Then, Sam crept downstairs into the kitchen and called Dr. Scott.

"Dr. Scott, I'm sorry to call so late," she whispered.

"No problem." His voice rang loud and energetic. "I just got back from a call. It never ceases to amaze me what animals can get themselves into. An Angus calf wiggled headfirst into a septic tank. Stunk something terrible. I took twenty dollars off the bill just so they'd let me take a shower before I drove home."

Behind Dr. Scott's voice, Sam heard electronic beeping. When she pictured Dr. Scott microwaving his dinner, she felt even more guilty.

Dinner at eleven o'clock at night, and she was about to add to his burden. Before she could, Dr. Scott guessed why she'd called.

"Probably nothing any of us can do about those mustangs, Samantha, but I thought I'd give you folks a try."

A scrap of loyalty kept Sam from saying her father was hopeless on this subject.

"Can't you just refuse to do it?" she asked the vet. "Gram said he told you to stand by. Maybe you could suddenly become unavailable."

"I could," Dr. Scott said. "But he might find someone else to do it, and maybe that vet wouldn't try to talk him out of destroying at least one or two of them."

"Have you seen them?" Sam asked.

"No. How bad are they?"

Sam thought a second, then decided there was no point in softening the truth. "They're not what most people would want to adopt, but I have an idea."

"Spill it," said the young vet, and Sam heard him take a bite of something.

"There's the tiniest possible chance I might know someone who'd take the horses."

"Who?"

"I can't say until I talk with her." Sam twisted the phone cord, then reached for Gram's personal phone book. She found a penciled-in number that looked like it had been written long ago. "If that guy Norman calls and says he wants you to put down the horses, please call me at this number."

She read the number written for Trudy Allen, then sighed. "Just ask for me."

The next morning, Dad didn't speak to Sam. She broke the silence by telling him she'd agreed to help Mrs. Allen with the horses' feet. For a minute, Sam thought he might say she couldn't go. Yesterday she would have applauded the decision. Today it would be disastrous.

"She's not having them shod, is she?" Gram asked as she sipped her morning coffee. "It's none of my business, of course, but it seems like a waste of money. Trudy never rides."

"I don't know, Gram. Getting her horses' feet worked on might be a sign she's interested in stuff outside her studio." Sam noticed that Dad still hadn't spoken. "I was pretty tired last night when I agreed to do it, but she said she needs me to hold Calico while the farrier trims her feet."

"Meaning the horse is a problem," Dad said.

Sam shrugged, but she thought both Dad and Gram were impressed that she'd agreed to help on a

Saturday, when she'd already done three hours of work for Deerpath Ranch every day that week.

And they hadn't said no, so Sam pressed her advantage.

"Gram, do you think you could drive me over there? Mrs. Allen said she'd give me a ride home, or if the farrier is coming this way, I'll ride with him."

Sam kept her expression casual and her fingers crossed. Gram had said Trudy Allen loved pintos. The group of unadoptable mustangs included several of them. If Mrs. Allen could be convinced she was their only hope, this plan might work.

Gram hesitated, looking at a huge wooden bowl sitting on the counter. It was filled with tomatoes. She must have some big cooking project in the works. Then, Gram met Dad's eyes and the decision was made.

"That's fine," Gram said. "Just let me start the tomatoes, basil, and garlic cooking down for pasta sauce. I'll bottle it when I get home."

Sweat glossed the farrier's brow and cheeks, dripping off his chin. He'd quickly discovered that Calico did not like having her feet handled, even by an expert.

"Are you sure you don't want to go to a twitch with this old girl?" the farrier asked.

Mrs. Allen, dressed in a denim skirt, white blouse, and straw hat, looked shocked. "Put that loop of chain on her tender lip and twist it, just so she won't fidget? I hardly think so."

Fidget was a mild word for Calico's lunging, kicking, and nipping. And though Mrs. Allen was the one answering, it was Sam who dangled from the halter rope, pulled off her feet by the mare each time the farrier approached her hindquarters.

Sam's hundred-pound body wouldn't stop the mare if she decided to run away, and the farrier knew it. He practiced the lesson Sam had been taught: Never turn your back on a horse, especially when you're handling its hooves.

The only good thing about Calico's bad behavior was Mrs. Allen's reaction to it. Her hair was pulled into an arm-thick braid. From the back, she looked like a young girl as she crooned baby talk to the pinto after the farrier finished his work.

She had a soft heart for horses, and that's exactly what Sam was counting on.

Still, she might not need it. Sam looked at her watch and a wave of relief washed over her. It was nearly noon and Dr. Scott hadn't called. Maybe Norman White had gotten over his urge to make a big decision.

As if her thoughts had triggered it, the phone inside Mrs. Allen's house began ringing.

"Don't know who that could be," Mrs. Allen said as she wrote out a check to the farrier.

"Shouldn't you answer it?" Sam urged.

If Dr. Scott was calling, the situation would be urgent. If it wasn't him, Sam could catch a ride home with the farrier, who had already packed his gear.

"It's probably someone selling something. My children only call on Sundays. Thank you," she said, handing the check to the farrier.

"Still—" Sam said.

"Or a wrong number." Mrs. Allen waved a hand at the house. "See? It's stopped already."

Sam led Calico toward her corral. The horse obeyed, sweet as a lamb, until they reached the gate. Then she balked, looking back over her shoulder toward the hills.

"It might have been for me," Sam mumbled.

"Why didn't you say so, girl?" Mrs. Allen sounded frustrated, but her expression was friendly as she watched Sam try to reason with Calico. "I can give you a ride home."

"Thanks," Sam said, but her mind was on those troubled horses, waiting miles away.

When she released Calico into her pen, Sam's arms felt limp. "Were you expecting Grace to call?" Mrs. Allen asked.

Sam shrugged as the pinto circled her pen at a trot. Ginger joined in. Then they both stopped short and faced the hills.

Calico's nicker was a gentle sound even the humans couldn't ignore.

"Calico, you're too old for such foolishness," Mrs.

Allen chided the horse. Turning to Sam, she explained, "That white stud is close by."

Sam managed to pronounce a single word. "Where?"

"Don't know, really. Some of those trails are set deep into the hills and cluttered with brush. If he gets up there among the trees, he's impossible to see. Only the horses know he's there."

Judge pawed and snorted.

"And they always let me know when he's around."

"Is it the Phantom?" Sam asked.

"Here now," Mrs. Allen clicked her tongue. "Don't tell me you still believe in that nonsense."

"Not really, but he —" Sam broke off as the telephone began ringing again. Of course it was impossible to tell, but the ringing sounded urgent.

"Go get it," Mrs. Allen said. "Maybe you'll get there before it stops this time."

Sam ran. She pushed through the iron gate, sprinted past the dying roses, and shouldered open the heavy wooden door. She'd pelted into the entrance hall before she had to stop and blink in the dimness.

Where was it? Where? A round table draped with a fringed scarf stood against the wall. The ivory-and-brass instrument sitting there looked like it might be an old-fashioned telephone. "Hello?" Sam shouted, not sure she was holding the receiver correctly.

"Sam? I thought I'd copied down the wrong number. Glen Scott, here," the vet rushed on. "Whatever you've got up your sleeve, it had better be good."

Sam's heart thundered so hard, she had to strain to hear.

"Norman White just called to confirm the request for euthanasia, plus one."

"Another—?" Sam started, but Dr. Scott talked right over her words.

"One of the unadoptable mares just produced a blind foal."

"Blind?" Sam felt dizzy.

"'Least that's what he says. I'm driving up to verify it and to put the whole bunch of them down. I hear ya," he said as Sam made a quiet moan, "and I'll stall, but he's got full authority, and if he's telling the truth about the way the mare's rejecting it, this baby could be a lost cause."

"I don't believe in lost causes," Sam shouted. The room got suddenly brighter as Mrs. Allen pushed the front door wider and stood listening.

"Well, good luck to us all, then," the vet said, "because Norman White told me he's already got a backhoe digging one big grave."

Chapter Nine ✑

"Dr. Scott? Dr. Scott!" Sam shouted, but the vet had already hung up. All she heard was the sound of her own voice echoing in the medicine- and tea-scented darkness.

Her knees felt weak. Sam held the edge of the round table as she hung up the telephone receiver. She wanted to sit down and get a grip on her feelings. She wanted to erase the mental picture of a huge black hole, just waiting for equine bodies. But there was no time for that.

"So you don't believe in lost causes?" Mrs. Allen sounded like she wanted to provoke a fight. "Does that mean you're dumb, or just impossibly young?"

"It means," Sam began, but then she stopped. She didn't know what to say. "It means that you keep fighting for what's right until there's no use anymore."

Mrs. Allen dipped her head in what looked like

agreement. "And how do you know when there's no point in fighting on?"

"When you're—when it's—when they're dead."

Mrs. Allen's head snapped back. Even in the dim hallway, Sam could see she was surprised. "Dead?"

Sam nodded and explained. "There's a temporary manager up at the Willow Springs wild horse corrals. He wants to kill a dozen mustangs, including"—Sam swallowed hard before she could go on—"a newborn foal."

"How can you be sure? This is probably just a rumor. I wouldn't worry, Samantha."

"It's no rumor. That," Sam said, pointing at the phone, "was Dr. Scott, the vet. He received an order to put them down. Today."

Mrs. Allen rubbed her arms, as if she was suddenly chilled.

"And you don't believe in lost causes?" she said with disbelief. "I'd say an order like that is proof of a lost cause. Government employees don't change their minds on a whim, you know."

"I know what it will take to change his mind," Sam said. "And it's more than a whim."

"I'm not sure I like the way you're looking at me, Samantha Forster. If you expect me to help, you'd better explain." Mrs. Allen shook her finger. "But don't get your hopes up."

"The horses he wants to kill have been labeled unadoptable. Some because they're old, others because they're ugly or have bad conformation."

Mrs. Allen looked dubious.

"It's true, Mrs. Allen. I wish it weren't, but it is."

"And how do you think I can help?"

"By adopting them," Sam said. "There's nothing else that will work. The rest of the horses have already been loaded on a truck bound for the Midwest. These are going to be put down and buried today."

"It's a terrible thing, but—"

"Please, Mrs. Allen," Sam begged. She ached as if someone tugged at her heart. "Their time is up."

Mrs. Allen's hand curled in a fist, and it covered her mouth as if she might cry. Then it dropped to her side and she looked angry.

"You must not be as bright as I thought you were, girl, if you can't see what the rest of the world does. I'm a useless old woman."

"You're not useless. You could save these horses!"

Sam wondered how an adult could be so wrong about herself. She started for the door, hoping Mrs. Allen would follow. She did, but not right away. Mrs. Allen stopped to scoop up her truck keys.

They were both standing on the front path when Sam made her final argument.

"You have new fences, plenty of graze, and a barn full of hay. You have everything those horses need, and besides that, you have"—Sam searched for the right word—"*nerve*. In fact, you can be a little scary."

The harsh winter sunlight showed every line in Mrs. Allen's face, but it also revealed her determination. Her chin came up with a jerk. Her brown eyes glittered, then narrowed.

Mrs. Allen blushed, and Sam was pretty sure her lined face colored with pleasure, not embarrassment.

"'A little scary'?" Mrs. Allen shook her head. "Very well, young lady, hop in the truck and tell me all I need to know about the man I'm going to scare."

Sam hurried toward the tangerine truck, telling Mrs. Allen everything she knew about Norman White. She crossed her fingers, hoping her plan would work.

It might.

Out of the corner of her eye, Sam considered Mrs. Allen. Beneath her fine clothes and tidy hair, she looked fired up for a fight. Though Sam had never met Norman White, she'd bet Mrs. Allen could take him.

Five minutes later, Sam had decided Mrs. Allen scared *her*. A lot. Gram might be a distracted driver, but Mrs. Allen drove as if she were queen of the roads and everyone else should just make way for royalty.

The truck bucked down the rutted lane at full speed. That was all right, since there was no one around until they reached a stop sign. There, the farrier had paused to make a left turn. Sam was staring out the window as Mrs. Allen drove right past him and the sign. She saw the farrier's jaw actually drop.

Things didn't improve from there. The traffic light just before the highway was red, and Mrs. Allen didn't notice. Or else—and Sam felt a bit queasy as she thought of it—Mrs. Allen just didn't obey traffic signs or signals, ever.

"They're going to put down how many wild horses?" Mrs. Allen asked.

She'd turned to face Sam, and the truck swerved toward the edge of the road. A few more feet and they would have plummeted down to War Drum Flats.

"Dr. Scott said six, but a dozen were supposed to be unadoptable, so I don't know what will happen with them."

Sam chattered like a chipmunk, trying to get the words out fast so Mrs. Allen would look back at the road.

"Ridiculous!" Mrs. Allen glared at Sam as if she were to blame.

Sam gestured toward the road until Mrs. Allen realized she had to correct the truck's path. She jerked the steering wheel so hard Sam's head hit the window.

Maybe that's what would happen when they reached Willow Springs, Sam thought. Maybe she'd discover she was hitting her head against a problem Mrs. Allen wouldn't solve. The old woman hadn't declared she *would* help, but she hadn't refused, either.

And Mrs. Allen had the freedom that only

belonged to adults. If she decided she wanted those horses, there was no one to tell her no.

Up ahead lay the sharp right turn to Willow Springs, and Sam hoped the tangerine truck made it in one piece. At this speed, maybe they'd beaten the vet.

"Where do I turn?" Mrs. Allen asked. "I've never been up here."

"Go right at that four-way stop." Sam pointed, and they not only made the turn, they survived the tricky part of the road called Thread the Needle.

"That's kind of a challenging drive, isn't it?" Mrs. Allen said as they pulled into the BLM parking lot.

Sam considered Mrs. Allen's color. She'd lost that flushed, ready-to-do-battle look and turned pale.

"Are you all right?" Sam asked.

"It took a little something out of me, but I'll rest later. Perhaps you can drive home."

Me? The word shrieked through Sam's brain, but she said nothing. Mrs. Allen had to battle Norman White. Everything else could just wait. Still, she wished she could get the old lady a drink of juice or something.

As they climbed out of the truck, a scraping sound froze them both. Far off, beyond the acres of pipe corrals, a backhoe labored in the dirt. Sam shivered. There it was, digging a mass grave.

Mrs. Allen brushed at her long denim skirt, retucked her white blouse, and touched her silver concho earrings. Then, once more, she lifted her chin.

They hadn't beaten the vet. Dr. Scott's van was parked beside the corral next to a wall of hay bales.

Oh, please don't let us be too late, Sam pleaded silently. There must be angels for horses.

Mrs. Allen touched Sam's arm, stopping her.

"I suspect he's the one we've come to see," Mrs. Allen's voice was low. She nodded toward a man who seemed to be ordering Dr. Scott around, though he only came up to the vet's shoulder. "Let's watch him a minute before we confront him, shall we?"

"I guess," Sam agreed.

He wore the same style of khaki uniform Brynna did, but Brynna just looked pressed and pulled together. This man looked like a little general.

"Nice to meet you, Dr. Scott. The animals are over here." He ushered the vet to the fence. "The mare is vicious. If she hasn't already killed the foal, she soon will."

"Mustang mothers are protective, Mr. White," Dr. Scott said.

So the little general *was* Brynna's heartless replacement.

"I think I know the difference between solicitous and savage behavior," he said in a mocking tone.

So why hadn't he separated the mare from the foal? Was he afraid the mare would attack him, too?

"I tell you," Norman White went on, "it would be a mercy to end them both. The young animal will be saved pain, and though the mare hadn't been slated for euthanasia, she's clearly mad. Just think if some unsuspecting adopter had ended up with her." He rocked back on his heels, looking pleased that he'd prevented a tragedy. "So, Dr. Scott, I hope you have enough medication for seven horses. I shouldn't think the young animal will need much."

Watching this man was like watching a horror movie, Sam decided. Norman White spoke with total conviction, just like a villain who thought he was right. No, more than that: he believed *he* was the good guy.

Sam thought she'd muffled her disgust, but she must have made some noise, because suddenly Norman White noticed them.

"I'll be with you folks in a second," he said, and flashed the sort of grin that made Sam wonder if he used the rodeo queen trick of putting Vaseline on his teeth to make his smile extra wide.

"I won't euthanize animals until I've examined them and determined their state of health," said Dr. Scott.

Was the vet raising his voice for Sam's benefit? Norman White tried to cover the unpleasantness with another phony smile.

"We have a little situation here," he said. "It would be great if you could wait in the office."

"Actually, we've come to"—Mrs. Allen paused as if she couldn't believe what she was about to say— "adopt a horse or two."

Or six? Maybe twelve? Sam tried to change Mrs. Allen's mind with the power of her own.

Now that they stood near him, Sam saw Norman White's name tag. He was no taller than she. He had the kind of muscular body that came from working out, not working.

The way he held himself—shoulders back, chest out, and chin high—made him look taller. His brown hair was cut in a military-short crew cut.

"I'll be with you soon," he said. "You folks can help most by just staying put." He winked. "Great."

Assuming they'd do as they were told, he nudged Dr. Scott away from the corral where the unadoptable horses were penned. Sam could see the animals inside, quiet and waiting. They were safe—for now.

The men walked toward a nearby corral and out of earshot.

"Kind of makes you want to salute, doesn't he?" Mrs. Allen said, nodding toward Norman White.

"No," Sam said. "He makes me sick. He wants to kill a newborn foal and call it a 'situation.'"

It would be one thing, Sam thought, if Norman White were trying to hide his feelings by acting calm. Jake did that all the time. So did Dad. But Sam figured if Norman White felt anything, it was an urge to tidy up a mess Brynna had left behind.

Surprised by the sudden warmth she felt for Brynna Olson, Sam realized the redhead was a strong ally, at least when it came to wild horses.

"I don't fancy being told to sit and stay, like a dog." Mrs. Allen looked after Norman White and the vet. "How about you?"

"No way," Sam said. Together, they followed at a distance, pausing beside the vet's van, where they could listen.

Sam could see the big paint mare. Her brown-and-white hide was stiff with sweat and smeared with dirt. Sam would bet the foal's birth had been difficult. The mare stood in the center of the corral, probably between her foal and the gate, although Sam couldn't see the baby.

The mare's head was lowered and her ears lay flat against her neck, warning all humans to keep their distance. When Norman White ignored her warning and leaned against the fence, the mare lunged forward. Then Sam saw why.

The foal lay in the corner of the corral like a crumpled quilt in shades of tan. The foal's forelegs were tucked under, and its head wobbled from side to side, as if scanning the corral in vain.

The mare's weariness had vanished. On full alert, her ears tipped forward. Her nostrils flared and closed, breathing the smell of enemies. Her eyes rolled to show the whites and her tail whipped side to side as the vet stepped on a fence rail to get a better view.

This time the mare didn't charge, because the foal moved behind her. As the baby made a little surge, trying to stand, Sam saw blood on its off hind leg.

The baby was definitely hurt and the mare had whirled to face it.

"There she goes again!" shouted Norman White, but Sam thought the mare looked concerned, not dangerous.

The foal made a piteous sound, and all at once Sam knew how the baby felt. She, too, had stared into the darkness and felt lost because her mother wasn't there.

Poor baby, Sam thought, but then the mare circled the foal, and ended by standing foursquare over it.

"That mare's not trying to kill her baby," whispered Mrs. Allen. "She's trying to save it."

The vet seemed to agree.

"I see the injury," Dr. Scott said, "but what makes you think the foal is blind?"

Norman White clapped his hands, then rattled the metal fence.

The mare lunged forward, teeth bared. Norman White was safe behind the fence, but the foal raised its head on its weak, trembling neck and its eyes were pale and blue. It gazed in the general direction of the ruckus, trembling.

He was right. The foal looked blind—and terrified.

Chapter Ten ∽

Dr. Scott was suddenly eager to approach the two horses.

"We'll have to put a rope on the mare and get her away from the foal. If I try to examine her baby now, she'll eat me alive," he said.

"There's no need for that," Norman White scoffed. "With a minimum of fuss you can put her down, then take care of the —"

As if he felt their glares, Norman White looked over his shoulder and spotted Sam and Mrs. Allen.

Dr. Scott shifted from foot to foot. He cared more about the animals than embarrassing Norman White.

"The Bureau of Land Management," the vet said, "does not put down healthy animals. Unless I'm convinced that mare and her young one are unsound, I'm not breaking that rule."

As if the vet had spoken a magic word, Norman White brightened.

"I'm a man who goes by rules, as well," he said, tapping his chest. "There are eight rules to consider in putting an animal down." Norman White began ticking the rules off on his fingers. "Incurable progressive disease, incurable transmissible disease, chronic lameness—" He gestured toward the pen of unadoptables. "We have several of those. Inoperable colic." He looked annoyed. "Not a problem at this time, but next comes foals with serious defects. I'm sure you'll agree blindness qualifies."

"I won't agree with anything till I've done an exam." Dr. Scott maintained a level tone, but Sam couldn't.

"I don't believe this," she whispered to Mrs. Allen. "He has *rules* for killing horses."

"I know his type," Mrs. Allen answered quietly. "Men like Norman White think they know what's best for everyone."

Dr. Scott studied the mare, judging how he could get past her to the foal. "I can already tell you there's been a misjudgment," he said. "I was worried when you called, because your description told me the mare already knew something was wrong with her baby. Nature can be cruel. She could have rejected her baby, but she didn't."

"Of course she did," Norman White said. "You can see the wound for yourself."

"I disagree. Look at her now. When the mare hurt the foal, she must have either gotten too close because she was assuring the young one she was near, or been trying to protect it from human interference."

"No, no, no." Norman White's lips snapped back in a mocking smile. "If you'd seen her display, you'd say otherwise. And that is one of the rules, you know. Animals with dangerous behavior traits should be destroyed."

Ignoring Norman White, Dr. Scott spotted the bearded man Sam thought of as Bale-Tosser and waved to him. Reluctantly, the man approached.

"Could you put a loop on that mare and reel her into the fence?"

"I've been trying to keep my distance," said Bale-Tosser. He sent Norman White a stern look. "But since it's you asking, I'll see what I can do."

Five minutes later, a rope flew out and a loop settled over the mare's neck. She flinched sideways, a brown-and-white mass fighting to stay with her baby.

Bale-Tosser wouldn't let her go. He cast one end of the rope over the top fence rail, passed it over again, and used the rail as a pulley to draw the mare nearer while Dr. Scott scurried toward the foal.

Startled by the skittering human and the unfamiliar smell, the foal gave a quick, high call.

"It's meant to sound that way," Mrs. Allen told Sam.

Sam noticed she'd covered her heart with her hand.

Mrs. Allen continued. "It's how small creatures

survive. They cry so pitifully, the sound just forces adults to come to the rescue."

As the mare bucked against the rope, Dr. Scott worked fast. His hands flew over the foal, feeling each bone and joint. When he'd finished, he tilted her head to the light.

He took his time examining her eyes. Sam searched Dr. Scott's face for a hint, but the vet's expression didn't reveal his findings.

Meanwhile, Norman White focused his worry on Mrs. Allen.

"I may have to ask you to leave." He twitched with impatience.

Mrs. Allen's set jaw and her hooded eyes indicated she wasn't going anywhere.

The mare reared, flinging herself against the rope just as Dr. Scott signaled to free her.

"Here she comes," Bale-Tosser shouted. He let the rope run through the loop and freed the mare.

Following her mustang instincts, she ran, head swinging from side to side, clearing a path to her baby even though there was no herd blocking her way.

She dropped her head and nosed the foal with such enthusiasm, the baby rolled onto her back. The snuffling reunion lasted only a moment. Then the foal struggled to rise and the mare gave a shuddering breath before facing the humans again.

"So, I was right, wasn't I?" Norman White asked.

"About the eyes?" Dr. Scott mused. "Probably,

but other than that the filly is healthy. None of the abnormally silky coat, rubbery hooves, or weakness you'd expect in a premature foal."

Norman White leaned forward as if he'd interrupt, but Dr. Scott didn't let him.

"The leg injury might make her a little slow to nurse, but my money's on the mare."

"What do you mean?" Norman White asked. "Can a man in your position afford to go soft?"

Sam heard the insult, so the vet must have, but Dr. Scott stayed cool and professional.

"Not at all," he said. "Look at this." Dr. Scott pointed.

The foal stood on shaking, golden legs. Gently, the mare used her muzzle to guide her daughter close enough to nurse.

"Take a look, Norm," Dr. Scott said.

"Mama's not going to take no for an answer," Mrs. Allen said proudly.

Frustrated, Norman White jammed his hands into his uniform pockets. "I've done the math on this issue. I've compared the costs of shipping these horses off to pasture against the cost of putting them down. I can save one hundred and twelve dollars per animal if the problem's dealt with here and now." He spread his hands out in a so-there-you-go gesture. "I'm not afraid to do what Brynna Olson won't."

Sam caught her breath. He sounded less like an adult than like a show-off kid. No wonder he was temporary. Who would hire a guy like this for real?

"So, folks, really." His voice grew tough. "You need to step into my office and have a soda or read a magazine while we take care of this. Then we'll find you a nice little horse."

Mrs. Allen planted her feet a bit apart. Her frown said she wouldn't budge. "Thanks for the offer, Mr. White, but we came to adopt a number of horses, those two among them."

Mrs. Allen shifted the big handbag she wore slung over her shoulder and met Sam's eyes.

Sam barely believed this was happening. She couldn't wait to tell Gram how Mrs. Allen had played fairy godmother to this bunch of hard-luck horses.

"You'd take on the responsibility of a blind foal?" Norman White looked confused.

"I might." Mrs. Allen clearly liked shocking the man. "I'm partial to pintos, you see. The mom is clearly a tobiano, and once she's cleaned up, I bet that filly shows herself a palomino pinto."

"Pintos," he repeated, as if he didn't quite understand what he was hearing.

"I know where there are even more. In that pen up there," Sam spoke up, pointed, then jogged toward the corral.

"Oh, no. Those animals are all losers. No one would want those horses."

Losers. Sam knew if she stood around and tried to educate Norman White, if she tried to explain the horses' situation, she'd end up yelling. That wouldn't help.

She glanced back to make sure Mrs. Allen was following her to the pen. She slowed down so the old lady could catch up. When had Mrs. Allen quit moving with an old woman's stiffness?

When Mrs. Allen fell into step beside Sam, she was muttering.

"What are you getting me into, girl?" Her tone was more amused than puzzled. Still, Sam couldn't take a chance that Mrs. Allen was reconsidering her decision to adopt lots of horses.

"I'll help you with them," Sam promised. "You can count on me, no matter what. And Brynna Olson has a blind mare. I know she'll help, too."

Mrs. Allen considered Sam carefully.

"Wyatt Forster's daughter with a good word to say about someone from BLM. That's something I never thought I'd hear."

Sam shrugged off the teasing and described her plan for the next week.

"I've been thinking I could sleep in your barn until we've got the filly nursing round-the-clock. Foals are supposed to drink their mother's milk up to seventeen times an hour," Sam explained. "Can you believe that? And just in case there's trouble with the mare, I'll be there."

All at once, Sam remembered the Phantom as a foal. Like many grays that paled to white as adults, he'd been born pure, midnight black. Because she'd been young herself, she'd named him Blackie.

He'd been a bundle of long legs and milky breath. Sam's arms could still remember the angular velvet feel of him as he'd let her wrap him in a hug.

Reality shattered the memory. Now he was a wild stallion, and Sam didn't know if she'd ever touch him again.

Still, her experience might help this blind filly survive.

"I had a foal of my own once," Sam said, "and I did a good job with him. Really."

Mrs. Allen motioned for Sam to hush, then she looked from the Roman-nosed chestnut to the sorrel's twisted legs and shook her head.

"This is a regular sideshow of sad horses." She took a deep breath and looked over her shoulder to consider Norman White.

He'd lagged behind to lecture Dr. Scott, and his gestures indicated he was astonished at the way things were going.

"Oh, well—in for a dime, in for a dollar," Mrs. Allen said. Then she must have caught Sam's look of confusion, because she added, "Or, I guess you might say, go big or go home."

Sam laughed, then sobered quickly as Mrs. Allen stared at Norman White once more. "I'll take every horse on the place before I let him kill them so that he looks like a good businessman. That's just not right."

Mrs. Allen turned with a quick movement that made her skirt swirl around her. "Mr. White?" She beckoned. "I'll take all of them."

"You can't be serious." He sighed, but his resigned eyes said he knew she was. "You'll have to fill out the forms, of course, and be cleared as an adopter."

Sam wondered why he didn't sound pleased.

"Ma'am, what on earth will you do with them?"

Mrs. Allen stared off at the horizon as if she saw something the others couldn't.

"I live on the edge of mustang country, and I've always had a mind to open a sanctuary for them. My husband hated the idea because our pastures were filled with cattle. Now the cattle are gone. Harold, God rest his soul, is gone, too." Mrs. Allen turned a silver wedding ring around on her finger, then smiled. "I just know he won't begrudge me my dream. Neither will you. Right, Mr. White?"

"No. But don't you want time to think this over?"

"I've had a lifetime on this range to think about it. My children are on their own and doing fine, but these pitiful creatures are not. I've got a little bit of money and a little less energy, but they're enough to help. I'm done wondering if I could do this. I *am* going to do this, right now."

Norman White gave a jerky nod, then gestured toward his office. "Come right along then, ma'am, and we'll get that paperwork started. In a few days"—he swallowed as if he had a sore throat—"the horses will be yours."

Everything was going so smoothly, Sam hated to interrupt, but she had to. "That little filly might not make it two days, do you think?" Sam asked, looking at Dr. Scott.

"Most foals who don't survive die in the first week of life," the vet agreed. "If, for some reason, the mare rejects that filly, someone must be on the spot to help her."

Mr. White rubbed his palm over his crew cut, looking stumped. "We're not set up to be nursemaids."

"You want to take them now?"

The question came from Bale-Tosser. He'd been so quiet, Sam had forgotten he was there. By the look on his face, he had a solution.

But how far could Mrs. Allen be pushed? Would she agree to take the filly and mare right away? Sam crossed every finger she could.

"It's not uncommon for us to foster out orphan foals," he continued. "This isn't much different."

"I'll do it," Mrs. Allen said slowly, "if Dr. Scott insists it's for the best. And if a certain young lady keeps her promises to help me out."

Norman White still wasn't satisfied. Using his index finger, he pointed at each mustang in the "unadoptable" corral, counting them up. "So, you want these horses, plus the mare and foal. All thirteen?" he asked.

Mrs. Allen hesitated before answering. "Oh, no, I can't do that, can I?" she said finally.

Sam bit her lower lip so hard, she thought it might bleed.

Dr. Scott cocked his head to one side as if he hadn't heard correctly.

Norman White chuckled, satisfied that he'd been right in thinking something was bound to go wrong.

"Thirteen horses would be unlucky," said Mrs. Allen. "So I'll trust the selection of number fourteen to you, Mr. White. Pick me one more, please. And make sure he's a real loser."

Chapter Eleven ❧

Sam and Mrs. Allen had a head start over the vet as they drove down the road to the highway.

"I'll drive you home, and talk with Wyatt and Grace if you like," Mrs. Allen said.

Sam was grateful Mrs. Allen felt tired, but not too tired to drive. Weariness made the old woman take each turn at half speed, and she slowed to a crawl through Thread the Needle and down to the highway that would take them to River Bend Ranch.

"You don't have to come in," Sam said. "You could catch a catnap in the car while I pack a few things and grab my sleeping bag. I'll only have them come talk with you if they give me trouble."

As Mrs. Allen smiled, a little of her fatigue appeared to fall away. Sam still thought the day had been too much for her. And it wasn't over yet.

Dr. Scott had agreed to move the mare and foal to Deerpath Ranch that evening. He'd said the pair needed as much quiet time as possible, so he'd wait until he thought they could stand the trip.

As soon as Sam got permission to spend the night in Mrs. Allen's barn, they planned to prepare a cozy stall for the mare and foal. After the two animals moved in, Sam and Mrs. Allen would have a long night of watching.

When they pulled into the ranch yard at River Bend, Sam noticed Dad's truck was gone. She sighed, glad he wasn't home. She'd been rude and childish last night. She owed him an apology.

But she wasn't ready to admit she'd been wrong. Besides, her backup plan had turned out to be the best idea, after all.

"I'll be right back, I hope." Sam sprinted across the yard, leaped onto the porch stairs, and burst into the kitchen.

The smell of homemade pasta sauce was incredible, but Sam ignored it. Instead, she began rattling off an explanation to Gram of why she wanted to leave when she'd just arrived home.

"That boy Darrell called again," Gram said before Sam finished. "This time he left a number."

"Oh," Sam said. "I'll call him back later. I've got to tell you what's happened since I left this morning."

This time, Gram didn't speak until Sam was through.

"Of course you can help out, but I don't want you in a stall alone with those mustangs." Gram followed

Sam up to her room. "Even a tame mare is unpredictable when she has a new baby."

Gram's concern inspired a sudden brainstorm.

Sam opened her closet and dug around until she found the "safety saddlebags" Gram had made her assemble when the first snowflake fell in the fall. The kit was packed with first aid supplies, a pair of winter gloves, dry socks, and matches. She was supposed to bring it along whenever she and Jen rode out alone.

"I'll take these, and I'll be careful," Sam said. That should have satisfied Gram, but when Sam looked up from folding a fresh shirt, she looked dubious. "I will be. I'm always careful."

"Samantha Anne, how *can* you say that with a straight face?" Gram hugged Sam's shoulders. "All the same, Trudy can use your help. Maybe this is what she needs to get back on her feet."

"Gram, is something wrong with Mrs. Allen?" Sam zipped her nylon gym bag. "Or is she just"— Sam shrugged—"you know, old."

Gram looked oddly amused before she answered.

"She's not sick, I don't think, it's just—" Gram broke off, frowning. "Trudy's art was always so important to her. She passed days and nights in her studio, painting, instead of spending time with her husband or children or friends. Seems like one day she just sort of woke up to find they were all gone and she was left alone."

"And you were her friend.. . . before."

"When we were girls," Gram said. "But later she didn't have time for me, and then . . . " She shrugged. "It's sad when friends drift apart, but it doesn't have to be permanent."

Gram looked surprised at her own words.

As Sam slipped her camera into her saddlebag, she reminded herself she really needed to buy a strap. The camera would be pretty well padded by the socks, but she should be wearing it around her neck. Mrs. Ely said disaster was never far away for something as delicate as a camera, and Sam had seen the truth of that firsthand.

She picked up her bag and felt ready to go.

Gram came with her. "Let me walk you out to the car, and I'll tell Trudy hello."

For days, Sam had worked at Deerpath Ranch, so cleaning out the box stall and filling it with fresh straw didn't seem odd. What did feel weird was entering Mrs. Allen's house for dinner.

Sam sat at a cluttered mahogany table as Mrs. Allen took TV dinners from a microwave oven.

"It's nothing like Grace makes, I know," Mrs. Allen said as she set the dinners beside two sodas.

"They look great." Sam meant it. Gram was so devoted to cooking hearty ranch fare, Sam rarely ate meals from cute little boxes. And she was never allowed soda with dinner.

For a few minutes, they ate in silence. Then a

grandfather clock bonged from somewhere in the house.

"Dr. Scott's certainly taking his time," said Mrs. Allen. "I hope everything's all right."

Trying not to worry, Sam concentrated on her dinner. After a few bites, she realized there wasn't much food in this clever little tray.

"Do you think the mare would rather be in with Calico, Ginger, and Judge, instead of alone in the barn?" Sam asked.

In a single scoop, Mrs. Allen spooned up the dessert from her dinner and savored it before she answered.

"She'd go off by herself if she was still with the herd," Mrs. Allen mused, "and not return until the little one was ready to face all the other horses."

For a minute, Mrs. Allen sounded like an expert. That reminded Sam of the wild horse paintings, cast aside in the art studio.

"You like mustangs," Sam began.

"I do, though it's almost illegal to say so around here." Mrs. Allen began clearing the table.

"So what about your paintings? The ones you did of horses?" Sam waited for Mrs. Allen to explain. She didn't. "Why are you working on that other stuff?"

"That 'other stuff' pays the bills," Mrs. Allen snapped.

Sam wanted to kick herself. When would she learn adults were touchy about money?

Mrs. Allen was sponging out her kitchen sink when she spoke again. "Mustangs were my favorite subjects until a few years ago. The work didn't sell, but that wild white stallion was just begging me to paint him."

Sam's mind went spinning. A few years ago, the Phantom had been pure black. Only recently had he grayed enough to look white by moonlight.

"Which white stallion?" Sam asked.

"Who knows?" Mrs. Allen leaned against the counter. "There's always been one on this range. I never wanted to know him. He should remain a mystery."

We must be completely different kinds of people, Sam thought. She couldn't imagine not wanting to know everything about the Phantom.

"I'd like to look at those paintings. Really look, this time. I kind of want to photograph wild horses." Sam waited for a polite way to tell Mrs. Allen about the front-page photo of Hammer, and about the Night Magic contest.

"You're welcome to look," Mrs. Allen said, but she didn't mention Sam's photographs. "I lost the urge to paint wild horses but not the urge to paint. Somehow, I turned to those hungry plants. They earn a nice profit," she said, tucking a lock of hair away from her face, "but I can't say they give me a reason to get up in the morning."

A neigh floated from the corral. Sam glanced out the window. Between the heavy velvet curtains, she saw darkness had fallen. Hooves churned up dirt in the corral and tires crunched on the gravel driveway. Dr. Scott had arrived.

Transferring the mare and filly from the padded trailer to the box stall was a snap.

Sam and Mrs. Allen stood on each side of the ramp, holding their arms straight out, and the pinto mare knew just what to do. She headed down the ramp and into the stall with the filly tucked tight against her side.

"All that corral time taught her something," Dr. Scott said as he bolted the stall door behind the horses.

"Brynna said those horses have been transferred between a bunch of different holding centers," Sam said. "I just can't believe how well the baby's doing."

Standing in a corner of the stall, the filly swung her head in a sweeping movement. Instead of seeing, she seemed to take in her new environment with flared nostrils and golden ears too big for her toylike head.

When the mare licked her with a big pink washcloth of a tongue, the filly toppled over. She seemed content, though, to stretch out in the straw and let her mother give her a bath.

"Have you named them yet?" Dr. Scott asked.

"The filly is Faith," Mrs. Allen said. Her eyebrows arched, as if daring them to call her sappy.

"For a number of obvious reasons."

Exhausted from their trip, the horses dozed. Faith slept with all four legs tucked beneath her and her chin on the fresh yellow straw. Her mother stood beside her, tail drooping, head hung low, with her eyes closed.

Quietly, Dr. Scott explained how he'd monitored Faith's progress at Willow Springs. She'd passed every test.

"She stood unassisted—without human help to get up on her hooves—in two hours, and nursed not long after. She did, and still does, have a little trouble finding the mare. That makes them both anxious, but it's to be expected."

The box stall was as big as most bedrooms. Sam closed her eyes and thought about trying to find something as big as a horse, blindfolded, in her own room. It wouldn't be hard, if the mare stayed still.

"We'll bell the mare," Mrs. Allen suggested. "I've got some jingle bells the kids used on a pony years back. They're stitched to a surcingle that went around the pony's middle when he pulled a sled for them." Mrs. Allen smiled at the memory. "I bet it would make a collar for her." Mrs. Allen pointed at the mare. "If she wears that, Faith can find her."

"Great idea!" Dr. Scott clapped his hands.

The mare snorted before her eyes were even open. She took a quick look around for danger, then dozed again.

Once they found the belled leather strap, the vet set to work.

Ears pricked forward to catch the unfamiliar sound of jingling, the mare was braced for trouble even before Dr. Scott opened the stall door.

Getting the collar over the mustang's head wasn't easy. Thirty minutes later, the vet was rubbing his shins and pulling up the cuffs of his jeans to see where the mare had kicked him.

"Looks like someone worked me over with a baseball bat," he muttered to the horse. "But we got that collar on, and now your baby knows how to find you."

Mrs. Allen walked the vet outside to his van. Sam pulled her fleece-lined jacket close and read over the vet's handwritten list of things to watch out for.

Sam glanced at her watch. It was only seven o'clock, but it felt like midnight. She was wondering where she should spread her sleeping bag when she heard another vehicle drive into Deerpath Ranch and stop.

"Evening, Jake," called Dr. Scott.

Jake? Sam buttoned her jacket and jammed her hands into her pockets. What was he doing here?

Jake was always protective of her, but tonight he'd have no reason to be. The mare's eyes were closed and her hind hoof was cocked and at rest. Faith sprawled on her side, almost hidden by the deep straw. There was nothing for Jake to worry about. Still, Sam had a bad feeling about his surprise arrival.

The barn's overhead lights made Jake's black hair shine. He wore a leather jacket open over a green flannel shirt. He limped as he came toward her, but he wore boots. Both boots.

"Where's your cast?" Sam blurted as Jake entered the barn.

"I cut it off." He said it proudly, limping less and strutting more.

"You cut it off? W-what did you use, a chain saw?" Sam heard herself sputtering, but Jake didn't answer. "Isn't the doctor supposed to do that? What did your parents say?"

"Mom was mad. Dad said if I broke it again I was on my own, so Mom's not speaking to him, either."

Faith rustled in the straw, and Sam lowered her voice to a whisper. "How can you smile about that, Jake?"

He shrugged, and Sam rolled her eyes. Only Mrs. Allen's return kept Sam from lecturing Jake on how many ways his decision was wrong.

Mrs. Allen's skirt had a smear of dirt at the hem and her white blouse had come untucked. Most of her hair had straggled loose from her barrette.

Jake sidled away, making room at the stall door for Mrs. Allen to peer in at her new horses. She wore a satisfied smile when she turned to Sam. "Did you notice she's a Medicine Hat?"

Sam looked at the gold-and-white foal. "I know that's some kind of pinto," she said, "but I'm not sure how you tell."

"They're horses with markings that were spiritually significant in some Native American tribes. You must know, Jake." Mrs. Allen tilted her head, waiting.

"My grandfather probably does." Jake's eyelids drooped, and Sam thought he was pretending to be bored. "I don't much believe in anything I can't see for myself."

"I wonder what Faith would say on that subject." Mrs. Allen gave the sort of smile that said Jake was acting like a typical teenager. "Well, you've both just encouraged me to tell you all I know," she said.

"See how her ears and the top of her head are dark gold? And her little chest has a dark spot in the shape of a shield? To some tribes those markings were holy."

"That's so cool," Sam said.

Jake muttered under his breath, but Mrs. Allen ignored him.

"Medicine Hat pintos were considered safe from enemies. They were ridden on important hunts and used in religious ceremonies, too.

"Like Faith, most Medicine Hats have white bodies, which make a nice canvas. The rider's painted symbols or handprints showed up brilliantly. That improved the horse's power, as well."

Jake rolled his eyes.

Mrs. Allen pretended not to notice. She yawned and blew the sleeping foal a kiss. "Poor little girl, I hope your special powers keep you safe."

The barn fell quiet, except for a pigeon cooing and preening on a rafter overhead.

"Well," Mrs. Allen said at last. "It appears these horses are in good hands. Samantha, I'm taking you up on your offer because I don't have much choice. If this keeps up, I may have to hire some help. It's been a long, hard day for an old lady like me. I'll leave my bedroom window open a bit, though. If anything goes wrong, run toward the house hollering and I'll meet you at the front door."

"I'll do that, Mrs. Allen."

Mrs. Allen paused at the barn door. "Even though your grandmother insists on manners, I think she'd agree it's all right for you to call me Trudy. After all, we're turning into partners, of a sort."

"Thanks—Trudy." Sam knew the name didn't sound natural coming from her, but she tried.

"And as for you, Jake Ely . . ."

"Yes, ma'am?"

"Thanks for coming over to help. Stay as long as you like."

Sam didn't groan. She didn't take back her new and improved opinions of Mrs. Allen, but why had the woman all but given Jake permission to take over? Because he was older? And a guy?

She and Trudy would have to have a talk. Later.

Right now, Mrs. Allen left the barn and crossed the ranch yard. It was minutes before Sam heard the front door open, then close.

Jake was *not* in charge, no matter what he thought. Sam wouldn't let him think he was. She crossed her arms and waited for Jake to explain why he was here.

He stared at the horses. He looked up at the expensive barn lights. He shifted his weight onto his good leg.

But Sam knew his game. She leaned against the stall door, relaxed. As she did, she smelled soap. Jake had probably showered before he drove over to Deerpath Ranch. Sam hadn't cleaned up since last night and she probably smelled like a horse.

That bothered her, but not enough to fall for Jake's strategy. He was waiting for her to give him an opening so he could jump in and scold her. But she would not do it.

When he set his jaw in impatience, Sam smiled.

If Jake was waiting for her to start up with him, he should have brought his sleeping bag.

Chapter Twelve ⌒

"𝒯HIS IS A BAD IDEA," Jake said at last.

Sam couldn't stay quiet anymore, either.

"You are so wrong, I don't even know where to start explaining."

"I can put up with the wild horse sanctuary," he began.

"Oh, wow. Isn't that lucky for Mrs. Allen?" Sam snapped. "What would she do if you couldn't?"

Jake drew up to his full height so that he could look down on her. "She should raise cattle. All over the country, houses and malls are covering ranch land, and people need meat."

Jake stopped while his contradictory feelings warred with each other.

"On the other hand, it's her land," he conceded. "But the sanctuary's too much work for a frail old lady. Even if she does hire some help."

"I think she can handle it," Sam said. She compared

the Mrs. Allen of last week, when she'd meandered out of the house to visit her horses, with the Mrs. Allen who'd faced down Norman White. "In fact," Sam said, her voice dropping to a whisper, "I think this sanctuary will keep her alive longer, give her something worthwhile to do, you know?"

Jake gave a shrug that might have meant "Whatever," except that he was kinder than that. At least that's what Sam thought—for another few seconds.

"The sanctuary's probably a done deal, but what the *heck* are you going to do with a blind filly?"

"Umm, I know! Keep her from dying. Yeah, that's it."

"No need for sarcasm, Sam."

"It's better than smacking you, which is what I'd like to do! Jake, up at Willow Springs, they had a backhoe digging a pit to put the bodies in!"

Behind them, bells tinkled. The mare stamped. She'd had enough of their argument.

"Let's step outside," Jake said.

Sam followed him. She didn't want to disturb the exhausted mare and sleeping foal, but she hated it that he was right. It was like he had to play the adult to her cranky child.

"What I should have asked was, what's the point of saving a blind filly? Just so she can live in the dark?"

"That's a mean thing to say."

"You know it's true."

"Not really. She's acting like a normal foal. She'll never know what she's missing. She's got her mom to teach her things, a herd of her own, and a warm stall to rest in. That beats being dead."

"I don't know, Sam. Think of how much trouble animals can get into."

As Jake knew she would, Sam thought of Buddy's escape from a corral and the calf's nearly fatal encounter with coyotes. She thought of horse fights and fires and floods. In every case, a blind horse would be at a life-threatening disadvantage.

"I've said all I came here to say. " Jake turned on his heel to leave.

Sam trusted Jake's opinion, but this time she didn't agree with him. Besides, swaggering away from a discussion was no way to end it.

"You came here because you're nosy," Sam argued, but when Jake kept walking, she knew her way of ending their fight was no better than his. "Jake, stop."

He didn't, so Sam tagged along, as she always had. She hoped Mrs. Allen was a sound sleeper, because the tagalong wouldn't mind yelling to set Jake straight.

"Do you think I should somehow not care about that filly?" Sam hurried to catch him. "Is that what you're saying?"

Jake passed his truck and headed toward the

lane, as if he was going to walk off his rotten temper.

Sam followed him down the lane. She couldn't help watching the tall weeds on either side. They were almost head high. Wind rushed past, rippling them so that it looked and sounded as if someone crept alongside her.

Sam lengthened her steps, trying to catch up. Even with a limp, Jake was fast.

"Just exactly how is it possible not to care?"

Still he didn't look back. Besides making her crazy, what was he doing? He'd almost reached the tree house.

Someone really ought to chop down these weeds. Darkness had fallen. She was getting an eerie Halloween feeling from being out here.

"The filly needs help, Jake. Would you abandon her?" Sam shouted. Suddenly, she stopped.

That's just what she'd be doing if she walked much farther. It was time for her to turn back to the barn and watch out for baby Faith, no matter what Jake did.

Sam had taken only a few steps in the opposite direction when Jake caught up with her.

"What?" Sam spun to face him.

Moonlight struck Jake's black hair. For the first time that night, Sam noticed he was hatless. With his button-front shirt instead of a tee-shirt, he would have looked nice if he weren't so angry.

"What is it with you?" he demanded. "You have

Ace, a nice, well-behaved horse who loves you, but you have to go chasing after the Phantom. You have Jen, a really good best friend, and you ignore her to hang out with crazy old Mrs. Allen."

Jake might be breathless, but he wasn't done yet. "You have *me*," he snarled, "a more tolerant friend than you deserve, but you have to start messing with Darrell."

"What?" Sam squawked. "You're nuts."

"Don't think I haven't heard—" Jake broke off and his eyes widened.

Behind her, the rustling turned to a sudden explosion of brush. Warm horsehide slammed Sam's shoulder. She stumbled, catching a glimpse of something white.

It was the Phantom. Like some kind of mythical monster bent on revenge, the stallion rushed toward Jake. The Phantom's head was lowered and his teeth were bared.

When his neck snaked from side to side, Sam understood. He wasn't attacking Jake. That was a herding motion. With a low neigh, he threatened Jake, telling him he'd better move away from Sam.

But Jake wouldn't be herded. He stepped aside so quickly, the Phantom passed him. Then, like a show-off matador, Jake gave the passing stallion a flat-palmed slap on the rump.

That was too much. When the stallion pivoted and faced Jake again, Sam could tell the touch had goaded the stallion beyond mere irritation.

Nostrils wide, head shaking the thick forelock from his eyes, the stallion struck out with a foreleg.

Jake froze, recognizing the move for a challenge.

"No!" Sam shouted.

She immediately hated what she'd done. The stallion startled back a step, soft eyes looking hurt that she'd called off his rescue.

That fast, it was over. One instant the Phantom was there. Then, in a fluid lunge, he bounded into the brush. It parted and he was gone.

Sam could hear herself panting in surprise and disappointment. "Thanks a lot, Jake."

For weeks she'd prayed the Phantom would remember she was a human he could trust. Then, as soon as he did, she'd shouted in his face.

"Sorry you had to choose between scaring him and letting him savage me," Jake said, but he didn't sound a bit sorry.

The barn was in sight now, and light fell in a golden rectangle from its door. Sam couldn't wait to get back inside, though she would have stayed out in the cold all night if she'd thought there was a chance the stallion would return.

Jake opened his creaky truck door. Then he called after her, quietly.

"You know all that stuff about Ace and Jen and me?"

"You were just mad, right?"

"No, but what I was trying to say is this: unless you really like having your heart broken, why don't you go with the sure thing, just once in your life?"

At two o'clock in the morning, Sam put aside the pencil and paper she'd been using to keep track of Faith's meals. Sam had had no trouble staying awake. Between guilt over neglected homework, worry over Jake's accusations, and the mare's restless pacing, she hadn't dozed for even an instant.

She'd decided tomorrow would be a big homework day, and Mrs. Allen would just have to watch over Faith on her own.

Then, Sam came to the conclusion that neither she nor Jake was wrong. Ever since her riding accident two years ago, when she'd fallen from Blackie and Jake had taken the blame, Jake had been too protective. So of course it seemed to him like she was always running after adventure.

And it was true that Sam couldn't resist the excitement of wild horses. Her heart soared at the sight of them, and nothing satisfied her more than helping them.

Not that she didn't love her friends. If Ace were here, she'd hug his neck and kiss his whiskery muzzle. She'd hug Jen, too. And maybe even Jake if he'd stand still for it.

But the important thing now was the mare and foal. Exhausted from her first day of life, Faith slept too deeply. She had to wake up and nurse. She needed the calories from her mother's milk to strengthen her new muscles.

The mare was restless. Her milk bag was swollen, and from her constant circling, Sam guessed she was uncomfortable.

"Poor mama horse," Sam whispered. "If you let me in there, I'll get her up."

The mare's deep nicker sounded like encouragement, but Sam hadn't forgotten Gram's warning. Mares with foals were unpredictable.

Sam grabbed a handful of sweet molasses grain from the feed room, opened the stall door, and sprinkled the grain in the manger.

Although it was exactly the same food, the mare seemed more interested in the grain that had missed the manger and fallen on the stall floor. She lowered her head, nostrils working, eyes fixed on Sam.

As the mare lipped the grain, Sam crept along the stall wall. She hoped the mare's year of captivity would keep her from charging.

Just then, a sound like pattering rain drew Sam's attention. The mare's milk was dripping into the straw and Faith needed every nutritious drop.

"Okay, girl," Sam crooned to the mare. "Since sleepyhead won't wake up on her own, I'll give her a little help."

The mare shook her head and stamped a hind hoof, but her nose still searched the straw for grain.

Carefully, Sam squatted next to the sleeping foal.

Beneath her honey-gold forelock, Faith's eyelashes fluttered. Her ribs moved as she sucked in a deep breath. Suddenly, her eyes opened. Sam went statue still. Then she remembered: even with her eyes wide open, the filly couldn't see her.

"Shhh," Sam said. If Faith squealed in alarm, the mare might panic. If she charged, Sam and Faith could both be hurt. "It's time for a midnight snack, baby. Past time."

Faith sighed, and her front legs rustled in the straw. Sam leaned forward to scoop her arms beneath the foal.

Just as she did, the baby figured out what she was missing. Her tongue darted out and licked Sam's cheek.

Sam's heart flipped over. Who could leave this trusting creature to die?

The mare raised her muzzle. Straw clung to her lips as she watched Sam with renewed suspicion.

Then, Faith's mouth clamped on Sam's nose.

Sam couldn't help laughing, but here came the mare! With one ear pinned back and her neck extended, the mare looked as if she hadn't decided whether Sam meant her baby any harm.

Gently but quickly, Sam detached the foal from her face and boosted her up on her tiny hooves.

"Right idea," Sam said, "but I'm not her. Can you hear your mom? She's coming."

Faith wobbled toward the bells tinkling on the mare's neck. The mare's head jerked up several times and she gave encouraging nickers, guiding the foal. Faith had taken only take three stiff steps when her nose collided with her mother's chest.

The mare gave Faith a hard nudge, urging her toward the milk bag, and in seconds both horses were content.

Feeling pleased, Sam walked out of the barn's warmth and into the night. *I'm only thirteen*, she thought, *and I'm saving a little life*.

The creepy feeling from earlier had passed. Now she didn't mind being alone in the dark, because she knew she wasn't.

The Phantom had proved that mustangs were nearby. Somewhere in the mountains, coyotes yipped. In one of the cottonwoods, an owl hooted, asking who was up wandering around. Overhead, Sam heard a silken rustling. She looked up to see a dark V of Canada geese, late on their migratory path and in a hurry.

A light brightened the round, stained-glass window upstairs in the house. Imp and Angel yapped a few times, then fell silent.

Even though it was her turn to sleep, Sam still didn't feel tired until Trudy approached and handed her a cup of hot milk sprinkled with nutmeg and cinnamon.

"Mmmm." Sam took a sip. "Thanks."

"You've stood watch more than your share," Trudy said, pulling on fuzzy gloves. "How are they doing?"

"Faith hadn't nursed in a few hours, so I got her up. Now they're both happy." Sam started to shiver, so she tightened her hands around the warm mug.

"I should ask if you were careful," Trudy said, "but you look fine to me, so I won't. Anything else going on?"

Sam was glad the night concealed her sudden blush.

"The Phantom was here."

"Ahh." Trudy sighed. "I haven't seen him in a long time. How does he look?"

Sam pointed at the moon, a sphere mottled with silver and white and gray. "Just like that. But I scared him away."

"I'm sorry. So, you didn't get a picture for your contest."

"No, I—I forgot to even take my camera out with me," Sam said. She couldn't believe she'd forgotten all about it, but she had. The camera was right where she'd left it, bundled inside the saddlebags in a corner of the barn.

"You know, when I had it in my head to paint them, sometimes I'd go up in the kids' tree house to watch mustangs. You can see a long stretch of the playa and there's a good view of the hot springs."

Sam had never seen hot springs at night. Most

weren't much bigger than a child's wading pool, but she could imagine one just on the horizon, reflecting the star-strewn night sky.

"And though the water's too warm for them to drink, I've seen mustangs wade right into it and play."

"No," Sam said, "not really." She'd never heard of such a thing, and certainly never seen it, but she wanted to believe it could happen.

Her mind conjured an image of a white stallion surrounded by ribbons of steam rising into the night. It would be too wildly beautiful for words. What if she could catch it on film?

"Why don't you grab your sleeping bag and climb up there?" Trudy encouraged her. "It's not as cozy, but you might see something worth seeing."

"I might see something incredible," Sam answered, and though she knew it guaranteed a sleepless night and a brain unfit for homework, Sam ran for her gear in the barn.

In minutes, she was climbing the pegs up to the tree house, camera sheltered between her sleeping bag and her chest.

Chapter Thirteen ℘

Sᴀᴍ ᴅɪᴅɴ'ᴛ ɢᴏ home on Sunday.

All day, she helped Trudy watch Faith and the mare, whom they had named Belle.

Sam petted and sweet-talked Judge, too. The old bay took the appearance of new horses as a challenge. To prove he was still the boss, he'd begun nipping at Calico and Ginger.

When Dad showed up at four o'clock in the afternoon, Sam hugged him around the burdens he was juggling. Though it had only been twenty-four hours, she felt as if she hadn't been home for a month.

"Dad! What's all this stuff? Boy, you won't believe what I've been doing. You've got to see Faith. She's incredible. A palomino pinto, and a Medicine Hat. You wouldn't know she was blind unless you, uh, knew."

Sam stopped talking.

In her last conversation with Dad, she'd been

rude, disrespectful, and downright illogical. All the same, he'd shown up with her backpack, fresh clothes, and a casserole of chicken and dumplings.

"Trudy said she could use you one more night." Dad nodded toward the violet Victorian house, where Trudy stood on the porch. "We said you could stay, with the understanding you did your homework and got to school on time."

Or else, said the set of Dad's jaw. Although he was granting her permission to do what she wanted, there would be serious punishment if she messed up.

"Yes, sir," Sam said as she took her backpack. "I won't let you down."

"Okay." He nodded. "I'll take a rain check on seeing the foal. I've got a date with that buckskin I've been working for you."

"Thanks, Dad."

Sam felt as if someone were cranking a spool of nerves tighter at the back of her neck. Dark Sunshine. Popcorn. Ace. Buddy. She was letting down all the animals that depended on her. She'd already let today slip away from her. She'd get home tomorrow, after school, and stay there, no matter what.

Behind her, Sam heard the black iron gate swing open. Trudy reached for the casserole dish, drew a deep whiff of the dinner Gram had sent, and closed her eyes.

"Heavenly," she said.

"Well, thanks for looking after our girl," Dad said.

"We're looking after each other. And a pitiful little scrap of horse flesh." Trudy watched Dad look down at his boots, his face shaded by his Stetson. When he didn't respond, she added, "I don't suppose you'd have any more use for that foal than my husband would have."

"Well, now, I don't know." Dad rubbed the back of his neck, and Sam knew he was embarrassed. But he didn't deny what Trudy had said.

Sam would bet her entire college fund and her camera that Dad agreed with Jake that the wild horse sanctuary was a silly idea.

"We'll be seeing you after school tomorrow," Dad told Sam. Then he touched the brim of his hat to Trudy and left.

A belly full of Gram's chicken made Sam too drowsy for homework. With her back propped up against a hay bale, she listened for signs of trouble in the box stall. Even that made her sleepy.

If Trudy could get her to school a little early, Sam knew she could slip into Mrs. Ely's classroom and do her algebra homework. Mrs. Ely always unlocked her classroom door an hour before the first bell, and algebra was really the only grade that would get Sam into serious trouble.

She yawned and set the alarm on her wristwatch

for six thirty. That would give her time to shower and change into the fresh clothes Dad had brought.

Sam touched the bulge of books in her backpack. She was behind in her reading for English, but she didn't feel very attentive. Besides, she liked that class and it shouldn't be hard to catch up.

When Faith blundered around the stall searching for Belle, Sam stood and watched.

"Over here, Faith," she called to the foal. "Oh, Belle—move, why don't you? Then she can tell where you are."

Belle swished her tail, but the faint sound wasn't much help to the filly. She gave a whinny of frustration. Then she tried rearing on her hind legs and toppled over sideways.

"That's what you get for your temper," Sam said.

She stood with her arms folded along the top of the stall door, wishing she could help. When Dr. Scott had come by this morning, though, he'd insisted mother and daughter must work out a system of communication by themselves. So Sam waited.

At last the foal simply collided with Belle's side and began drinking. Faith's fluffy caramel-colored tail twitched from side to side, making her look like a wind-up toy.

Once she'd finished her meal, Faith lay in the soft straw, legs tucked beneath her. Sam decided it would be safe for her to doze, too.

Of course, then she wasn't sleepy, so she went

outside. She even strolled down the lane, listening to the whisper of wind through the weeds, hoping the Phantom would come to her again.

He didn't.

As she walked back to the barn, she heard a commotion. That was Faith's squeal, and the sound of hooves on wood must be Belle kicking the stall. Sam broke into a run.

As soon as she came into the barn, she saw Faith had jammed her chest into a corner.

"Oh, no!" Sam couldn't help but cry out.

Belle was trying to help. She nudged from behind, attempting to turn her baby. But Faith thought her mother was urging her forward into the darkness. The filly's front hooves scrabbled where the walls met, trying to climb.

"Stop, baby, stop!" Sam opened the stall door and Belle rushed at her, teeth bared.

Last night's acceptance hadn't lasted long. Sam closed the door. She raced to get more grain. She tossed it into the stall, but this time the bribe didn't work.

Faith battered her chest against the wood. Soon, she'd cut herself—or fill her tender skin with slivers.

"Try this. Get it on Belle and I'll hold her while you turn Faith around." A nightgowned Trudy stood at Sam's elbow with a lariat. Sam hadn't even heard her come in.

"I'm not very good," Sam began.

"She doesn't need very good," Trudy snapped. "She needs very fast."

It took Sam three tries, but she roped the mare, slipped through the stall door, and wrestled the thrashing foal out of the corner.

"Hold her!" Sam yelled. Belle lunged against the rope with pinned ears and a menacing look in her eyes.

"Just get out of there!" Trudy gasped, and Sam could see she was about to lose her grip on the rope.

Sam made it, but only because of Faith.

Even as Belle shook free of the rope, Faith pushed past Sam. Faith's tiny ears swiveled, then pricked forward, catching the sound of the bells. She jumped forward, ran into Belle, then nursed furiously, as if she thought she'd lost her mother for good. Every so often, Faith gave a little grunt, then glared at the people she couldn't even see.

Trudy rubbed both hands over her face. "What on earth made her do that?"

"She was lost," Sam explained. "We need some way to tell her she's coming to a wall."

"Or we could put them in a big pasture."

Sam winced at the idea. "Then Faith would have a terrible time finding her mother."

"We'll think of something." Trudy shook her head and sighed. "I bet you wish you were home in bed."

Mentally, Sam gave herself a quick once-over. "No," she said. "I like this more. Why don't you"—

she had to break off to stifle a yawn—"go on to bed. I've set my alarm, so if you don't mind driving in, I'll be ready."

"I'll be down here at seven thirty, all right?"

"I'll be up at your house for a shower long before that," Sam said.

And she would have been, Sam thought later, if she hadn't slept through her wristwatch alarm.

She was dreaming of riding a skateboard down a cobblestoned San Francisco street, way too fast, as she slowly came awake and realized Dr. Scott was looking down at her.

"Hi, Sam." The vet reached up to turn off a light switch, since the barn was flooded with morning sun. "Didn't expect to see you here."

Heart thundering, Sam looked at her watch.

"Seven thirty! It can't be seven thirty! I have to be at school at eight and I haven't even taken a shower!"

"You still have time, if you don't mind being a little late," Trudy said from the barn door.

"I can't be late. Dad will kill me if I get a tardy." Sam ran into the tack room, slammed the door, and snatched off her soiled jeans and sweatshirt.

I won't let you down. Had she actually said that to Dad yesterday when he'd stared at her as if he expected the worst? Yes, she had.

Sam pulled on clean jeans, zipped and snapped

them, then grabbed the sweater Dad had brought her. Where had this come from? Then she remembered. This ribbed turtleneck had been a present from Gram. Sam never wore it because it looked terrible on her. The burgundy color made her auburn hair look sick. And it was too tight.

Outside, the tangerine truck revved up.

"She's a terrible driver," Sam hissed to Dr. Scott as she burst out of the tack room, shoving her dirty clothes into her backpack. They didn't fit, but where else could she put them?

"I know," he agreed. "Give me twenty minutes to look at mother and child." He nodded toward Faith and Belle. "I have to go back up to Willow Springs, and I'll take you in as far as the bus stop."

"Too late," Sam moaned as Trudy honked the horn. And then the yapping began. She looked at Dr. Scott with an expression of horror. "Those dogs . . . "

"Imp and Angel," he supplied calmly.

"I can't ride to school with them."

He gave an oh-go-on wave of his hand. "They're tiny dogs. You'll all fit."

That wasn't what Sam meant. But she couldn't tell Dr. Scott, who'd never met an animal he didn't love, that Imp and Angel were her personal version of hell hounds.

Chapter Fourteen ✧

SAM WAS PRETTY sure she looked like a kidnap victim, the way she threw herself from Trudy's truck as it rounded the corner into Darton High's parking lot.

The combination of Trudy's driving, the two bouncing Boston terriers, and her tardiness was almost more than Sam could take.

The first bell was ringing as her feet touched asphalt. The late bell would sound before she could make it to her locker.

Skip the locker. Run to history. But there was Jen, just about to enter her own classroom directly across the hall from Mrs. Ely's. Jen's mouth formed an irritating but perfect O.

"Are you all right, Sam?"

"Don't ask!"

"Where'd you get this sweater?" Jen extracted a piece of straw that had been stabbing Sam's back during the entire ride from Deerpath Ranch.

Sam stared at it. She'd imagined it much larger and she would have pulled it out herself, except that she couldn't. Trudy driving normally was scary. Trudy driving fast made you think of ambulances. Sam hadn't been able to release her grip on the door handle long enough to feel around for the straw.

But wait. Jen had said something. . . .

"What's wrong with this sweater?" Sam demanded.

"Nothing. I've just never seen it before."

"You're looking at me like I have the fashion sense of a . . . a . . . a llama!"

Jen sputtered with laughter, then shook her head. "No, it's fine. It just doesn't look like something you'd pick out."

Sam couldn't admit that her father had selected her clothes for the day. She didn't, but just the sight of Jen's concern erased Sam's irritation. She was lucky to have such a friend.

Sam slung an arm around Jen's neck and gave her a squeeze.

"We'll talk later, okay?"

"If you say so," Jen said, but she seemed awfully eager to escape.

Sam sniffed at the air around her and really hoped she didn't smell like a horse.

The tardy bell was ringing when Sam dove toward her seat. Her backpack caught on an empty desk and pulled it over with a crash.

It was Rachel's desk, but Rachel was still across the room, being worshiped by one of her fans. At Sam's arrival and the ensuing chaos, the older girl flowed back toward her seat.

Coffee-colored hair curved in a casual wing across Rachel's brow, and her lips shone with a perfect shade of gloss. She wore low boots, slim-fitting pants, and a fancy silk shawl that should have looked silly. It didn't.

As Sam righted the desk, she felt Rachel taking in her disheveled appearance.

"Good morning, Sunshine," Rachel purred.

Everyone laughed.

Sam wished she were the sort of person who could drop Rachel with a head butt, right where she stood. Instead, she tucked herself into her seat and tried to arrange her notebook before Mrs. Ely entered the classroom from her office.

Rachel batted at the air in front of her nose. "What did you do, sleep in a barn?" she joked.

Sam froze. What should she say? Rachel didn't know she'd hit on the truth. Sam managed a tight smile, then flipped her fingers through her short auburn hair to give it some shape.

When one of Sam's nails encountered a tiny green piece of alfalfa, Rachel saw.

"You did!" she crowed. She covered her mouth and shook her head so that her hair flipped from side to side in a silken rush. "You *did* sleep in a barn. Oh, my God!"

"Welcome to Monday morning, class. Homework up to the front of the rows," Mrs. Ely ordered as she stepped into the room. "Rachel, settle down."

Jake's mom was an unlikely rescuer, since Sam couldn't remember being assigned any homework on Friday. She had no papers to pass up. Still, she felt relieved. The last time she'd asked, she was earning an A minus in this class, and anything was better than being ridiculed by Rachel Slocum.

Well, almost anything.

"Since so many of you asked for them, I'm passing out grade checks," said Mrs. Ely. She walked down the rows, distributing computer printouts. Pausing next to Sam, she said under her breath, "This surprised me."

Sam looked at the slip of paper and saw that her grade in history was a C.

After class, Sam filed out the door to find Jen waiting for her. "We got grade checks today. How 'bout you?" Jen asked.

"Yeah," Sam said, and held it up for Jen to see.

"Well," Jen said, as they headed for P.E., "it could be worse."

In English, it was.

And in algebra.

By lunchtime, Sam had nearly decided she'd

rather go back to San Francisco than go home and tell Gram and Dad about her grades.

At least she wouldn't go hungry. She'd arrived at school without lunch or money, of course, but Jen had taken pity on her.

"Two *D*s and a *C*," Jen said, repeating the grades Sam had just announced.

Sam took a bite of her half of Jen's peanut butter and jelly sandwich. "I knew about algebra, but I love English!"

"You said you didn't read all the stories," Jen pointed out.

"I read most of them. Miss Finch just wasn't impressed with my ability to fake it." Sam tried to joke, but she was worried. Gram and Dad would definitely punish her. That would probably mean time away from the horses.

"You need a plan, Sam, and organization is one of my strong points."

"Are you offering to help me?" Sam asked. "Assuming, of course, Gram and Dad let me speak to another living soul?"

"I will, but you've got to promise not to keep doing all this extra stuff. Don't give me that bewildered look. Show you a lost cause, and you're all over it," Jen scolded. "You know what I'm talking about."

"Sort of." Sam searched her brain for excuses, but even there, things swirled in a mad clutter. The HARP horses, her ranch chores, the mustang sanctuary, Faith, school. But none of those were lost causes.

Sam took a long drink from Jen's soda, hoping to silence her. It didn't work.

"You can't do everything," Jen said. "You're only one person. You need to prioritize. Decide what's most important and do that first."

Sam let Jen's words sink in, soothing her like a warm shower. She was almost feeling hopeful—until she looked past Jen to see Darrell leering from behind her.

Jen turned to see what Sam was watching. "What does he want?"

"Brain surgery." Sam swallowed the last bit of her part of Jen's sandwich and remembered what Gram had said Saturday afternoon. "He's been calling my house."

Jen covered Sam's hand with hers and pretended to be sincere. "Don't encourage him, honey."

"Yuck!" Sam snatched away her hand. "Never."

But then she remembered Jake's flare of jealousy and took a second look at Darrell.

He wasn't leering, really. In fact, there was something very un-Darrell-like about his expression. In spite of his baggy pants and backward baseball cap, he looked serious.

"I should probably go see what he wants." Sam stood.

"Sam, you may want to seek professional help if

you take this one on." She jerked her thumb toward Darrell.

Sam just crossed her eyes in response before walking away.

Darrell beckoned her toward a quiet corner of the lunchroom.

"Didn't you get my message?"

"I was really busy. What's up? Is it something about Jake?"

Darrell looked confused, then disappointed.

"Well, no. It's an exposé for the school paper. See, I heard about this secret"—Darrell paused and spun his hand in the air—"thing, and I thought you could write about it for the newspaper."

In spite of her doubt, Sam was curious.

"What secret thing?"

"I don't know if I should tell you here."

The bell rang.

"Darrell, I don't have time for drama today. I can't be late to journalism." She started toward her locker and noticed he fell into step beside her. "If you don't count P.E., it's my highest grade right now."

Why in the world had she just told him that? Sam wanted to suck the words back into her mouth. What if he told Jake?

"Okay, this is it. You know Kris Cameron? Sure you do." Darrell snickered when Sam stopped with her locker half open. "You just got the same gooey look every other girl in this school gets when his name is mentioned. Forget it."

Darrell slammed Sam's locker door.

Curiosity overruled Sam's aggravation. "Tell me," she insisted as she dialed her combination all over again. "Do it now, Darrell, and make it fast."

Darrell slipped a small slip of yellow paper into Sam's hand.

She looked down at it. "A blank hall pass," she said. "So?"

"Take a good look at it. See where the attendance secretary's signature isn't exactly clear?"

Sam looked. He was right.

"Okay, here's the deal." Darrell stepped closer and lowered his voice. "Kris Cameron and some of his jock buddies don't see anything wrong with using counterfeit passes."

"What?"

"No squawking," Darrell whispered into her ear. He stood close enough that Sam was glad she'd had a chance to shower in P.E. "Sheesh, I don't mind ratting on rats, but I thought you could keep it quiet."

"I can," she whispered back.

"They're printing these up and giving them to their friends. Are you sure you can keep me out of this?"

"Absolutely. A good journalist protects her sources." Sam stopped, and Jen's voice echoed in her mind. She didn't need any more projects. "But you should be the one to take this to the principal."

There. It felt good to turn something down.

"Forget it," Darrell said, and he weaseled his finger into her hand, trying to recapture the fake pass. "Ms. Santos would just think I was part of it. I have a history, you know."

Sam's hand closed tighter, with the pass inside. She used her other hand to shove Darrell away. "I'll see what I can do about it."

"Yeah," Darrell said as he moved away. "Well, don't strain yourself."

Sam stuck out her tongue. *How mature*, she was thinking. Boy, she was even sick of herself.

She'd taken about three steps when she saw Jake watching her. His brown eyes cut across the crowded hall as if they were the only two people in it.

So what if he'd seen her whispering with Darrell? And if their hands had been fumbling together, it was really no big deal. There was a perfectly logical explanation. She just couldn't give it to him, not right now.

Moaning, Sam swerved into journalism.

Peace, at last. Or, if not peace, at least she knew what she was doing in here.

The classroom was already crowded with students. Some were typing stories. Others sorted through photographs. Rachel and Daisy were trying to bully all Darton *Dialogue* reporters into selling extra ads to local merchants.

"We want a big issue, with color pictures, for Prom," Rachel was saying. "The only way we can afford that, is if you get out and sell ads."

Sam collapsed into a desk and let the class swirl around her, trying to think. Meditation didn't last long, though.

"Hey hotshot," Mr. Blair said as he loomed up beside her. "Did you give up on being the first-ever freshman editor?"

The journalism teacher had encouraged her and coerced her into doing her best work in the class. He wasn't content to let her pass the textbook quizzes and take a few pictures. And one other thing about Mr. Blair—he always used a loud, booming voice to keep students in line.

"No," Sam said, hoping against hope that her lowered voice would influence his. "I haven't given up."

"The evidence says otherwise. RJay practically rewrote your last story, and you haven't exactly been begging for photo assignments. You don't get to be an editor by just showing up."

Most of the other students moved away or lowered their eyes. They'd been in the same position, and sympathized with Sam. Only Rachel put her hand on her hip and gave a gloating smile.

Sam tried not to not get upset. She had too much to do. She could tell Mr. Blair what was going on in her life and maybe he'd back off. Or she could show members of the school's ruling clique that they couldn't get away with stuff just because they were popular.

"Oh, and you should have seen the little cowgirl

when she showed up in history this morning," Rachel chirped to Daisy. "At least now it looks like she got the manure off her shoes."

Sam tried to keep her lips together, but it was a losing battle. "Actually, Mr. Blair, I'm working on an exposé."

"You are, huh?" Mr. Blair considered her. "Normally, I'd say that was an excuse. But I'll trust you for it."

Sam sighed. Deadline wasn't until next week. By then, she'd have her life in order. Jen had promised to help.

"Sounds like it might be a big story," Mr. Blair mused, "so it will need extra work. This is Monday. Get me a rough draft by Wednesday. Got it, Forster?"

"Sure, Mr. Blair," Sam said. "That ought to be just fine."

Chapter Fifteen ❧

AT LEAST ACE loved her.

Sam set aside the rubber curry comb she'd been using and slid her hand over the gelding's gleaming red-brown coat.

The mustang's weight shifted. He leaned into the touch of her hand as if he couldn't get enough affection.

"You don't care about bad grades, do you, boy?" Sam circled the warm brown neck with her arms and leaned her cheek against him. Ace was just the right size for her hugs. "You don't notice how I'm dressed, and you don't even know what it means to be cool."

Sam stepped back. Ace peered through his coarse black forelock and bobbed his head. "Actually, I don't think you'd care that I'm definitely not cool, and about to do something that will ruin my prospects for ever being that way."

Ace bobbed his head again. Even when she

started the comb through his long, black mane and hit a snag, he didn't flinch away.

"They're not going to ground me," she told the horse. "In fact"—Sam glanced toward the barn door—"the only rules are that I can't stay over at Trudy's on school nights, I have to make a plan for all the stuff I want to do and get their approval, and I have to get someone to help me in algebra."

Ace blew through his lips and stamped a front hoof before giving her a hard nudge.

"I'm not complaining," she told him. "Or were you adding another condition? Do I need to ride my favorite horse more often?"

Sam glanced at her watch. Five o'clock.

Since she'd been home, she'd already collected eggs and shooed the chickens into their coop for the night. She'd folded a mountain of laundry and chopped onions, garlic, and chili peppers for the enchiladas Gram was making. She'd tried to take Buddy for a walk outside the pasture, but the half-grown calf had fled as if the rope Sam held were a snake.

"Wanna go, boy?" Sam darted into the tack room and took Ace's bridle from a hook. "If we went on a bareback ride around the ranch, you'd behave, wouldn't you?"

Once more, Ace considered her through his black forelock. This time mischief glowed in his eyes. Ace hadn't been out of his corral for a ride in days. She'd better stay on her toes.

Outside the barn, it was cold. The sky looked gray and metallic, like the hubcaps on Gram's old Buick. Dusk wasn't too far away.

Ace wanted to jog, but she kept him at a walk so the wind wouldn't pierce her fleece jacket any more than it was already.

"Need to dress for the weather," called Dallas, River Bend's foreman, from his chair on the bunkhouse porch.

"Yeah," Sam shouted back.

"Good to see you home for a change," he added.

Sam waved, and circled the ten-acre pasture. Strawberry and Tank followed along the fence. Dark Sunshine and Popcorn kept more distance between themselves and the fence as they watched Sam and Ace.

But Dark Sunshine must have gotten too close for Strawberry's liking. All of a sudden, the red roan wheeled and ran at the little buckskin.

Dark Sunshine didn't run. Head high, legs braced, she waited for Strawberry. The older mare slowed to a trot, then curved her big body to lash out with her hind hooves.

The mares exchanged whistling neighs along with kicks and a few nips, but neither seemed victorious. After a few seconds, both shook their shaggy manes and lowered their heads, searching for sparse November grass.

"I guess that's how it's done, Ace," Sam said.

All horses nipped and kicked, but they rarely attacked a superior animal. Among horses with the same ranking within the herd, spats didn't last long. She'd seen that in the wild, and right here in the pasture, too.

Sam watched the horses and wondered if it was the same for humans. If Dark Sunshine had shied and run away, Strawberry would have bullied her again tomorrow.

"Like she does you." Sam patted Ace's neck. And yet Ace got along fine with Trudy's horses. "Maybe it has to do with reputation, too," she mused. "Judge, Calico, and Ginger don't know you're too nice for your own good."

After all, it had taken Hammer, a stallion from far away, to challenge the Phantom.

Sam knew there was a pattern; she just couldn't quite grasp it. While she was trying, Ace grew restless, pawing the dust as he waited for Sam to do something.

His head swung around and he nipped at Sam's boot.

"Hey!" she shouted. "Just because you're bored doesn't mean you get to take a bite of me."

She tightened her reins and made Ace weave between the cottonwood trees. She was careful to keep him at an even trot.

As she rode back toward the barn, Sam noticed Popcorn and Dark Sunshine standing together, heads high. Their nostrils were open, testing the icy wind. Sam wondered what they smelled.

Not the Phantom, or Ace would have been sniffing, too.

Whatever it was, the two mustangs turned, hooves thudding, and galloped across the pasture. At the edge of a grassless patch, the sound of their hooves changed to a brittle hammering, and they swerved away from a low spot that often collected rainwater and froze. Even though it wasn't icy now, the horses remembered that sound.

"I've got it!" Sam shouted. Ace's ears tipped back to catch her voice, but his gait stayed steady. It was a good thing, too, because Sam could hardly wait to get back to the house and call Trudy, and she didn't have time for a fall.

Dad was on the telephone when Sam came into the kitchen. She hung her fleece jacket by the door, pushed her windblown hair from her eyes, and rubbed her hands together.

"So, that's the way it is with her," Dad was saying. His eyes flicked up to meet Sam's.

He must be talking to Brynna. Maybe Aunt Sue. Whichever one it was, Sam knew she was the "her" Dad meant. She could tell it wasn't good, either, by the way he turned his back to continue his conversation.

"Out to Deerpath. Yeah."

Okay, Aunt Sue wouldn't know Deerpath Ranch, so it had to be Brynna.

Sam peeked in the oven. The enchiladas were covered with red sauce and golden cheese. Her mouth watered. She closed the oven door and gave Dad's back an impatient stare.

Couldn't they talk lovey-dovey after she'd told Trudy her plan for saving baby Faith from hurting herself?

Dad turned, holding out the telephone receiver. "For you," he said.

Sam stared at it. She didn't especially want to talk to Brynna if the BLM woman was just trying to score points with Dad by being nice to his daughter.

"She wants to talk with you about the horses."

Sam's pulse pelted against her wrist as she reached for the telephone. What if something had gone wrong and Trudy couldn't adopt the raggedy mustangs at Willow Springs? What if Norman White had gotten his way after all?

"Hello?" Sam dropped the receiver before Brynna could answer, and Dad scooped it up and delivered it into her shaking hands. "Sorry." The static on the line said Brynna was still in Washington, D.C. "How are you?"

"I'm fine, since you found those mustangs a miracle." Brynna's voice was full of affection and maybe a little respect. Sam felt warmth spread down to her toes.

"Oh, you mean Trudy Allen," Sam said.

"I do. You did a wonderful thing, for the horses and for Mrs. Allen. The few times I met that woman, she seemed bitter and, I don't know, lost. You've done a good deed."

Sam didn't know what to say.

"Thanks," she mumbled.

"I'm wondering if your dad agrees." Brynna's voice held a drop of amusement.

"I don't think so." Sam looked up to see Dad watching her. His squint said he thought they were conspiring against him.

"I bet the Elys and the Kenworthys will feel the same, but we'll deal with it. "

Sam felt good. Much as she disliked Brynna's crush on Dad, there was a lot about her that Sam admired.

"The main thing is to make sure those horses stay put once they get to Deerpath Ranch," Brynna continued. "I've been thinking. If they were tired out when they arrived, they might settle in better and make a good start."

Sam imagined the horses jammed into a truck. It was a short trip from Willow Springs to Deerpath Ranch, but Sam wasn't sure what Brynna had in mind.

"What's the weather like right now?" Brynna asked. "The Internet report says cold and clear."

Sam was even more confused. She looked at Dad,

stirring something in a pot on the stove, then she looked toward the window. "That's right, but it feels like it could snow pretty soon."

"Not tomorrow?"

Sam shook her head. How weird that she'd gone from a San Francisco schoolgirl to a rancher's daughter who could predict the weather by how it felt on her skin. "Not tomorrow," she agreed.

"I wonder if you and the Ely boys and Jen . . . " Brynna's voice trailed off as if she were weighing the idea. "What do you think about a horse drive?"

"Oh, wow."

"It's only about twenty miles. It could be a hard day's work if any of them decide to make a break for the range, but they're all wearing government freeze brands, so if you had to gather them up later, you could. Think it would work?"

"I do." Sam knew she had to be honest, though, so she added, "I'll see if I can get the others together, but I don't know if I can do it. I've got problems at school."

Dad clanged the lid back on the pot he'd been tending.

"Let me talk with him," Brynna said.

"Okay. Dad, she wants to talk to you again."

Now it was Dad's turn to worry before accepting the phone. "You two are team-ropin' me, aren't you?"

Sam shrugged as he took the receiver.

The conversation lasted long enough that Sam

was able to explain everything to Gram when she came downstairs to check her enchiladas, rice, and beans. They pretended not to listen as Dad argued with Brynna.

At last he hung up. Thumbs hung in his pockets, he stared at the kitchen floor.

Sam stayed quiet. She was in no position to negotiate.

"Well," Gram said, "if she does everything we told her to this afternoon, are you going to let Sam go on this wild horse drive?"

Sam jumped, startled by the fact that Gram was clearly on her side. Gram, who was always so protective. How had this happened?

"Of course I am." Dad kept staring at the floor. "With you three against me, I've got no more chance than a cottontail at a coyote convention."

He looked up finally, rubbing the back of his neck. "Now, when's dinner?"

Chapter Sixteen ❧

Sam waited until Dad had served himself a third enchilada to ask what he thought of her idea.

"Faith keeps running into the stall walls and scuffing herself up."

"This is the blind filly?" Gram asked.

"Yes. Trudy named her Faith," Sam said.

"Trudy, is it?" Dad asked, eyebrows raised.

Sam shifted in her chair. "She asked me to call her that, since we've been working together."

"Go ahead," Dad said.

"I was thinking we could put some kind of different footing just before the stall wall to act as a signal. You know, like maybe cedar chips. I think Trudy has some in her garden shed. We could layer them a couple of feet out from the stall wall." Sam showed them with her hands. "And when Faith heard and felt her hooves hit them, it would alert her."

"I think that's a fine idea," Gram said, then turned

expectantly to Dad.

"Might work," he said.

"Brynna has a blind horse, too," Gram reminded them. "You might get some ideas from her."

Dad pushed his plate away, though he didn't appear to be finished.

"I will. And, since I don't want Faith to get hurt any more than necessary," Sam went on, "after I'm excused from the table, may I please call Trudy and tell her my idea?"

Sam tried to sound polite. She was hoping Dad or Gram would offer to drive her over to Deerpath Ranch so Trudy wouldn't have to do the job alone.

No one did, though, even while she was talking on the phone and explaining. Before she hung up, Gram interrupted.

"Samantha, tell Trudy if she'd like some help doing it, I've got no plans this evening."

Surprised because Gram rarely went out at night, Sam repeated the suggestion. While they both waited, Sam could tell more was at stake than just a neighborly offer. Gram was trying to rekindle a friendship.

"Tell her that would be just great," Trudy said.

Sam repeated Mrs. Allen's words, and Gram smiled.

"Tell her," Gram said, "to put on the coffeepot, because I'm bringing over some brownies made with Mexican chocolate."

That night, Sam worked on listing her priorities, then she called Jen to read them aloud.

"This is a pretty honest list," Sam said.

"You know how stuntmen always warn people, 'Don't try this at home'? I'm not sure you should have tried this without me, an experienced planner, by your side."

"Jen . . ." Sam rested her head against the wall.

"Shut up?" Jen guessed.

"Just listen." Sam paused. When there was no interruption, she went ahead. "My first priority is the ranch. That includes Gram, Dad, and my friends—especially you and that idiot Jake."

Sam was putting a check mark next to that first item when Jen cleared her throat.

"I'm not sure I understand how Jake and I fit in with the ranch."

"Jennifer Kenworthy, I put you on this list and I can cross you off it," Sam threatened.

"Okay, okay, go ahead."

"Number two is school."

"Good," Jen said. "And if I can give you one tiny piece of advice? Go see those teachers who are giving you low grades."

"How embarrassing," Sam said. "I can't do that."

"Then write them letters. But whatever you do, let them know you're taking those grades seriously. Okay?"

"I'll do it, but I won't like it." Sam fluttered her

list so Jen could hear it. "Three is Ace and the HARP horses. They're really number two, and school is number three, but Gram and Dad wouldn't like that. "Number four is Trudy, the mustang sanctuary, and Faith, the blind filly."

"Is that all?" Jen asked.

"Isn't that enough? You were the one telling me to cut down on my, you know, commitments."

"Yeah," Jen said, stretching out the word into three syllables.

"What did I leave out?"

"Other than the Phantom?"

"The Phantom is under number one," Sam explained patiently. "With friends and family."

"Of course. Anything else?" Jen was fishing for something, but what? "No thug matters?"

Sam let the words ricochet around in her brain, but they made no sense.

"Huh?" she asked.

"You know, something to do with Darrell . . . "

"He's not a thug. He's Jake's friend."

"I knew you liked him," Jen said in a singsong voice.

"I don't!"

"What were you guys whispering about in the hall then?"

"I can't tell you. It's a secret. And don't even bother acting like your feelings are hurt," Sam warned. "It's about school."

"Well, he sure doesn't want you to tutor him in algebra."

"Hey!"

"Sorry, sorry." Jen's voice was muffled, as if she was holding her hand over the receiver. "Yes, Mom. Okay. Sam, I have to get off. My mother has instituted a totally arbitrary nine o' clock—" Sam heard sharp words in the background. "Gotta go."

Smiling, Sam was about to carry her list in to Dad when the phone rang. It was Gram. She was laughing.

"Tonight, *I'm* going to stay at Deerpath Ranch. Trudy and I are having a slumber party out in the barn."

"Really?" Sam couldn't believe what she was hearing.

Could someone be holding Gram hostage and making her say this? It wasn't likely, but neither was the slumber party story.

"Yes, really," Gram said. "Let Wyatt know, so he doesn't think I've run off the road and ruined the Buick."

"Okay, Gram," Sam said. Dad was already leaning in the kitchen doorway when she hung up the phone.

"She staying over at Trudy's for a while?" he asked.

"All night!"

Dad shook his head. "I've had enough for one day. I'm going to bed."

"Dad, could you maybe just look at my list first?" she asked, holding out the paper.

He snatched it quickly, as if he were angry she'd asked, and Sam's hopes plummeted. He spent such a long time reading it, she wondered where she'd gone wrong.

"How did you grow up so fast?" he asked finally.

"I guess I couldn't help it," Sam answered, knowing that sounded lame.

"This is a good list. You can miss classes and go on that horse drive Wednesday—under two conditions."

"Anything," Sam said.

"First, you notify all your teachers what's going on with you." He paused when Sam nodded. "Next, you promise to stick to it."

"I will, Dad."

Still holding the list, Dad tapped it against his palm. "Most of it's not a surprise, but I'm wondering how you came around to caring about Trudy Allen so much."

Sam let out a long breath. "It was the way she took on Mr. White when he wanted to kill those mustangs. She was polite and all, but she stood up to him. Before that, I didn't understand how she could love her horses and still neglect them. But now, I'm not sure she could help it."

"You don't think she was out of her head or something?" Dad asked.

"No. I think she was really depressed about her kids and husband being gone and she just sort of forgot what the horses needed. Now she's pretty cheered up, she has all that fenced land, and Gram's her friend again. I think she'll stay on top of things."

"We'll make sure she does," Dad said. "Now, you get on up to bed."

"See you in the morning!" Sam called as she trotted up the stairs. Even though she thought it was too early for sleep, sometimes it was smart to quit while you were ahead.

The day of the wild horse drive dawned blue and white, and so cold Ace refused to leave the barn.

"C'mon, boy," Sam coaxed. "Here they come."

Sam heard the stock truck rumble over the River Bend bridge. The truck belonged to the Elys. Jake's brother Nate had agreed to drive from the Three Ponies Ranch to River Bend and the Gold Dust, collecting the saddle horses he'd take up to Willow Springs.

Jake and two of his brothers were driving there in a pickup, and Gram was driving Sam and Jen up in her old Buick. Even though she no longer thought Gram was the worst driver in the county, Sam wished she could ride with Ace.

The gelding took a step, then shook his head and lagged at the end of his reins.

"Don't be balky," she scolded. "You know you'll have fun."

Ace might crave the warmth of civilization now, but he was still a mustang. Today he'd get to stampede across the range with a herd.

"You'll thank me later," Sam said as they moved toward the truck.

She wore a jacket and wool gloves. She'd pulled on long underwear before her jeans, too, and considered wearing the neon orange muffler Aunt Sue had knitted. But she'd ended up stuffing it back in the drawer. It was just too gaudy, even if it was warm.

Nate lowered the stock truck ramp and Ace walked right in. Of the three horses already inside, only Witch, Jake's black saddle mare, kicked and protested Ace's arrival.

Witch had a right to be skittish. Jake hadn't ridden in weeks. Today he'd be back in the saddle. Of course, Sam had told Jake that he was crazy. Today promised to be a three-hour rodeo. But Jake had given her his tomcat grin and said, "Yeah, won't it be cool?"

She hadn't really expected him to say anything different. She didn't know a single cowboy who worried about staying in one piece.

" 'Bye, Ace," Sam said as Nate bolted the stock trailer gate. "See you up there!"

Norman White paced on the porch outside the BLM office at Willow Springs. If his long woolen coat was supposed to make him look taller, it failed.

His boots clumped as he walked back and forth in front of the six teenagers holding their horses' reins. They all wished he'd hurry up.

Gram would say Norman White was nervous as a cat. Sam guessed he just hated bending rules.

"Of course, Mrs. Allen has signed the adoption papers on these horses," he said, fidgeting with the fringed ends of his scarf. "And, as you know, she received a special permit to herd these horses to Deerpath Ranch instead of driving them in a truck."

He looked bewildered and likely to babble on for hours, so Sam took mercy on him. And the other riders. She stepped forward.

"We're all experienced on horseback and we've all herded, Mr. White. Last night we even got together and had a strategy session. Each one of us knows what to do. Nate's riding point, in front. I'm riding drag—way in back. Everyone else is ranged along the sides."

"But the terrain is rugged," Norman White warned.

"And each one of us was born on ranches between here and the Deerpath spread," Jen put in. "So we know all the canyons and coulees and the places where playa can turn into quicksand."

"Really, sir," Nate said respectfully. "This is a pretty short ride for most of us. We've all been on weeklong drives."

As if he agreed, Nate's horse Digger, a brown

gelding with a white chin spot, raised his head and whinnied eagerly.

"Our horses know their jobs, too," Jen added, patting her mare's arched neck. Sam had never seen Silk Stockings, the palomino Jen called Silly, so calm and ready to work.

"All right then," Mr. White said with a resigned sigh. He pointed toward the big pen. "Good luck to you."

Within seconds, the riders were lined up.

Sam thought she'd burst with anticipation when the gate was opened and swung wide.

The Roman-nosed gelding came first. Caution showed in every line of his body as he slipped through the opening. He tested scents on the icy air, and then his walk became a trot. He'd been fooled before, and he noted each horse and rider with a nod, but he moved on. The other mustangs crowded after him.

The dirt road lay before them. Their path went up the hill, then down to the highway. It was clear and as safe as humans could make it.

Gram had parked at the foot of the road leading up to Willow Springs to block other drivers. Not that there would have been many at seven o'clock on a Wednesday morning, but the horses had already been given their second chance at life. No one wanted them to lose it.

Like a multicolored raft, mustangs and riders

drifted through Thread the Needle. No horse made a break for freedom.

It was a good thing, Sam thought as she glanced over the cliff to the steep, rocky incline. Once she'd galloped Ace down there, with the Phantom running alongside. Rocks had slipped, shale had shattered. Only the horses had been having a good time. Sam never wanted to ride that breakneck hillside again.

When dust and motion signaled the herd's approach, Gram moved her Buick to block the highway.

At the first clack of their own hooves on asphalt, the mustangs shied. The ill-tempered black tried to jump the two-lane highway. When he failed, the herd turned back on itself.

Crooning in the same low voice he used with cattle, Jake removed his black Stetson and waved it. He looked happy and at home. His movement was so natural, none of the horses panicked.

The tall bay with white socks swerved away from Jake, then darted across the highway. All the others followed, lifting their hooves in high, prancing steps.

Even from the back of the herd, Sam enjoyed their grace. She liked riding drag. As soon as they crossed this road, she'd have time to appreciate the terrain they rode over. Even now, during winter, the sagebrush-covered hills rolled all around like a gray-green ocean.

When the other mustangs had crossed and only

the sorrel with twisted legs remained on her side of the pavement, Sam clucked quietly. Through a veil of flaxen mane, the filly studied Sam, then trotted ahead and paused to peek through the passenger's window of Gram's car.

"Hello, there," came Gram's voice.

Curiosity satisfied, the filly moved after the herd. Watching her, Sam was glad some BLM wrangler had taken the sorrel off the range. Her unsteady gait would have attracted predators, and the filly couldn't have outrun them. She would have ended up feeding a den of coyotes or a mountain lion.

Now, the filly was on her way to safe pasture, where she would be almost free again.

Ace fought the reins, anticipating a gallop across War Drum Flats. She and Jen always gave their horses their heads here, and Ace knew it.

He barely glanced at the shallow lake centered on the flats. He wasn't thirsty and neither were the mustangs. He saw no reason to go slow.

In fact, the herders had agreed last night that this would be the place to let the mustangs enjoy their first run.

Nate lined out his brown gelding ahead of the herd, and Sam caught the sound of his yipping as he urged the gelding to race away with the other horses on his heels.

All the riders leaned forward, smooching and clucking to the herd. In minutes, the ground shook with the thunder of many hooves, and the riders could barely keep up. As one, the paints, chestnuts, and blacks realized they could gallop with no fear of a helicopter turning them back. Hoofbeats, grunts, and neighs echoed all around Sam.

Suddenly, a wild, high neigh rang from the rocky cliffs. Ace answered it by running faster.

With the wind whipping tears from her eyes, Sam chanced a look up. The clouds were so heavy with snow, only their edges were teased into wisps by the howling wind.

Hooves rumbled all around her, growing louder, surrounding her. Sam felt a jolt of confusion. She was supposed to be last in line. All of the horses should be ahead of her.

Fingers clenched around her reins, her fist resting against the saddle horn, Sam looked back to see if other mustangs had escaped their pens and followed.

They hadn't.

The Phantom was galloping after Sam, closing the gap with each stride. He surged like a thundercloud ready to explode. Sam leaned forward in her saddle, holding tight from instinct. Everything around her spun in a dizzying whirl. Only her heart stood still, as Ace swerved hard to the left, bucked, and fell into step with the Phantom.

Chapter Seventeen ☙

ᴀT FIRST, SAM PULLED her reins snug, reminding Ace of the bit in his mouth.

Her place was at the back of the herd and she meant to stay there, even if she wanted more than anything to follow the stallion.

Ace had no such devotion to duty. He set his jaw against the bit. When Sam exerted more pressure, he flexed his neck, working hard to escape its pull.

The stallion surged ahead. Although he ran about ten feet out to her left, Sam thought she knew what he had in mind. She must keep the Phantom from stealing the herd.

She loosened her reins, letting Ace run, and the gelding vaulted forward, straining to run side by side with the stallion.

If the Phantom tried to cut out mares and take them, Sam had to be there first. She'd force Ace between the stallion and the herd.

For several breathless minutes, they galloped along the banks of the La Charla. Even if he succeeded in cutting out some mares, the Phantom would have to herd them across the river, and that would slow him down. She'd try to stop him, of course, but part of her would love to see them go.

Suddenly, the Phantom moved closer. Muscles slid and stretched under a silver hide that looked like satin. He couldn't be more than five feet away.

His warmth and nearness swept Sam's mind free of responsibility. More than anything, she wanted to slip from Ace's back to the stallion's. She wanted to lean close to that mane that was rising into the wind like white flame. She wanted to feel its texture against her cheek and cling there as he carried her into the mountains.

She couldn't ride him, and she knew it, but the Phantom was near enough to touch.

The last time she'd smoothed her hand over his skin, he'd been drugged and filthy, unconscious in the dirt at the rodeo grounds. Now he was himself, running free and within reach of her fingertips.

Sam could not resist.

Her hand had just grazed the sleek blend of neck into shoulder when Ace felt her weight shift. He followed the cue he'd been given, swerving left and colliding with the Phantom.

Sam was falling, gasping, tipping loose from the saddle. Brown and white equine legs flashed before her eyes with blurred and dizzying speed. The desert floor—tan, green, gray, and studded with rocks—rushed toward her.

Sam's legs tightened convulsively. She jammed her boot toes deeper into her stirrups. If she fought the momentum of each step heaving her forward, she could fling herself back and avoid pitching facefirst off the racing gelding. Grabbing a handful of Ace's mane, ignoring the pain of stretched tendons, she pulled herself upright.

Panting but centered in the saddle, Sam could hardly believe her eyes when the Phantom began taunting Ace, asking him to play.

The mighty stallion frisked like a yearling, running and bucking, flashing his heels at the sky.

No one's looking. Sam realized she was the only one watching the stallion. It was like magic, as if the two of them were invisible. He leaped a big clump of sagebrush, tucking his front legs, letting his back legs trail in a graceful line toward the earth.

Zanzibar. She didn't call out to him, but she used the stallion's secret name in her mind. When she was an old lady, she'd have this picture in her brain. No one else had seen Zanzibar running for pure joy.

Only when he put on an extra burst of speed and veered toward Brian Ely did another rider notice him. Brian did a double take and pointed. They kept the herd running, but other riders turned to look.

And then he left them.

He ran like the wind, passing the other mustangs. He swept by Silly, who slowed in awe of the stallion and nearly sent Jen flying over her palomino ears. Unchecked by the admiration, the Phantom passed Jake on Witch, then flaunted his tail in the face of the Roman-nosed gelding.

Leaping like a carousel horse, the Phantom rocketed past the lead horse. Nate's brown gelding didn't have time to sprint before the stallion cut right, sweeping in front of him.

After that, everyone watched as he splashed across the river, pulled himself up on the far bank, then shook a rainstorm of water from his bright coat.

The riders worked to control the herd, refusing to let them follow the stallion as he found a trail into the foothills, took it over a dozen stairstep mesas, and vanished.

In front, Nate slowed and so did the herd. Then the outriders turned the horses toward Deerpath Ranch.

Once they reached the ranch yard, Jake kept a paint from turning toward the barn. Jen sent Silly to brush back the cranky black gelding when he tried to follow, and then the horses stampeded toward the open land ahead.

The riders pulled up. Trudy held the pasture gate open, and the mustangs funneled through the opening into the huge, newly fenced pasture that lay waiting for them. The sorrel filly was the last one through.

Dressed in wide black pants and a jacket that looked like curly red lambswool, Trudy closed the gate and bolted it.

"Welcome home," she called to the horses. Wind snatched at the ponytail clamped at the nape of her neck as she leaned back against the fence and faced the teenaged riders.

"Thank you."

A chorus of voices indicated the drive had been fun, not a chore, and entirely too short.

Saddle horses milled. Riders gave each other smiles and high fives, and still no one mentioned the Phantom.

An old-fashioned triangle jangled from somewhere, and Trudy pointed the riders toward her house and a huge ranch breakfast.

After the riders had finished cooling out their horses, they crowded into the house. Even blindfolded, Sam would have known Gram's cooking. Platters of home-fried potatoes smelled of crisp onion, deep bowls of scrambled eggs were garnished with crumbled bacon, and pitchers of orange juice and mountains of corn muffins filled the center of Mrs. Allen's dining room table.

It was barely noon on the best sort of holiday. Everyone else was in school and they weren't! The whole day stretched before them, and once the huge meal had taken the edge from their appetites, they lounged back in their chairs and sipped the hot chocolate served as dessert.

"So, was I seein' things or was that the Phantom?" Brian Ely looked around the table.

"Yeah, that was him," Jake said, and other voices agreed.

Sam held her breath, and Jen stiffened in the chair beside her, but no one turned to question her.

"Was he trying to steal mares, do you think?" Trudy asked as she and Gram cleared empty dishes from the table.

"No offense, Trudy, but I hope not. Those mares are not prime pickins for any stallion," Gram said, and laughter covered the rest of her sentence.

"He didn't make much of a try," Jake said.

"He didn't want 'em or he could've taken 'em," Nate said. "Don't ya think?" He watched the table for nods. "Who was gonna challenge him, that old chestnut gelding? I don't think so."

"He was just chasing along for the fun of it," Brian said.

The idea made Sam smile. Brian was right. The Phantom had suffered beatings and confinement in Karla Starr's rodeo company. She'd turned him into a man-hater, nearly a man-killer, but the stallion had survived, and now he rejoiced in his freedom.

"And he didn't give a hoot about us," said Brian.

"That's because he's the king out there," Jen said. "Men are of no consequence on the range."

"Women, either," Brian put in.

Jen pushed her black-rimmed glasses up her nose, then continued patiently. "We were on his turf, and he was literally running circles around us."

Even Jake gave a grudging nod, and Sam allowed herself a single comment. "He was just letting us know that he's *back*."

Snowflakes drifted from clouds that blotted out the sky by the time all the riders started for home. Sam liked riding in the snow sometimes, but right now she was glad she was done riding for the day.

When Nate offered to drop Ace at River Bend so that Sam could ride home later with Gram, she almost hugged him.

Afternoon quiet hung over the ranch by the time Sam and Trudy walked down to see Faith.

It was only Wednesday. She'd wakened in sight of Faith on Monday morning. Still, Sam felt she'd been away from the blind foal for much too long.

But she didn't feel the clutch of guilt she had last night, as she'd worried over the foal. She knew Faith was in good hands, even if they weren't her own. Since Sam had seen the Phantom, whole and happy, something inside her had changed.

Out in the pasture, the snow was piling up fast. It was light and fluffy, and the mustangs' hooves thudded as they investigated their new home.

"I want to show you something," Trudy said, gesturing back toward the barn. "Your cedar chip idea worked just fine," she said as they crossed the ranch yard. "So I did the same thing in the paddock. See?"

Around the paddock's fence line, Trudy had made a gravel border. She'd poured gravel in a circle at the base of two small trees, too, so Faith wouldn't collide with them without warning.

"Have you tried it yet? Can we turn her out?" Sam asked.

"I have, and she loves it. But she's never been out in the snow. Hear her fussing?"

Squeals of frustration turned into sniffing delight as Trudy opened the box stall door and released Belle and Faith. The gold-and-white filly ran two bucking laps around the enclosure. Her delicate hind legs launched twisting kicks, and momentum made her broadside Belle.

To escape, the mare bolted for the open stall door, but it slammed in the wind, and she turned, resigned, to tend her lively daughter.

The mare nibbled Faith's little fluff of mane, and the foal protested with a rear. She didn't want to stay still for a minute. Faith backed away, out of Belle's reach, and then she stopped.

At last, she'd noticed something different in the air.

For a minute, the foal trembled. Then she lifted her muzzle as high as her short neck would allow.

"She feels the snow," Sam said.

Faith blinked white eyelashes, and her sightless blue eyes stared at the clouds. Sam pitied the filly, until Faith stuck out her long pink tongue.

"She's catching snowflakes!" Sam clapped her hands in delight.

"Isn't she precious?" Trudy slipped her bare hands into opposite sleeves and sighed. "And to think, that monster of a man wanted her dead."

Without speaking, they turned toward the fenced range where the other mustangs were settling in. All of them grazed at the farthest edge of the pasture-lands.

Trudy shaded her eyes, as if that would bring the horses into focus. "Right now, you can't tell which of those dark dots are horses and which are rocks or sagebrush. But by the next time you come over, they'll all have names."

"That'll be fun, naming them all," Sam said.

"This whole project is fun, and it feels good," Trudy said. "In fact, would you think I was crazy if I tried to work something out with Brynna so that I could take more unadoptable mustangs?"

"Crazy? I'd think you were wonderful," Sam said. "But I don't know how much acreage they'd require you to have."

"I've been thinking about that, too, and I wonder if I could get Linc Slocum to sell back the property I sold him right after my husband died."

"I knew it was him," Sam grumbled. *It always is,* she thought, but she didn't say it. Instead, she looked back out at the pasture, which was slowly turning white.

A loud slam made both of them jump.

"I've got to get a new latch installed on that door." Trudy nodded toward the paddock. "Sometimes it blows shut and it near scares me to death."

Sam gazed back at the big pasture. She thought she could pick out the chestnut stallion.

"I think those lucky horses are going to love living here," Sam said, and she caught Trudy's satisfied smile.

"And I'm going to love having them."

Belly-down on her bed, Sam studied. She'd been at it for over an hour. She had two tests the next day.

Sam let her forehead fall on her literature book. What if the faculty room wasn't really a place for teachers to eat lunch and grade papers? What if they got together in there and planned to make all of their exams fall on the same day?

Sam propped her cheek on her palm. If so, Mrs. Ely was out of the loop. The history exam was on Friday.

At least Gram had exempted her from kitchen chores. That meant no television or phone calls, but the trade-off was okay. She had to get great grades on these tests or there was no telling what Gram and Dad would do.

Twenty minutes later, Sam closed her literature book. She'd read everything, gone over the questions at the end of each story, and written down guesses for the essay question. She was good to go in English.

She tackled algebra next, but one niggling thought kept her from concentrating.

Where was that scrap of paper Gram had given her Saturday? She searched her room and finally, under a pair of jeans, Sam found it. Yep, there was Darrell's number. Now she had to work up the nerve to dial it.

Sam padded downstairs in her socks. Gram and Dad were watching television.

"I have to call somebody for journalism," she said. "You can listen if you want."

Dad's gaze shifted from the television. He took in her rumpled sweats and the pencil she was twirling, and nodded.

"Go ahead," he told her. "Even prisoners are allowed one phone call."

Darrell was surprised to hear from her, but he didn't like what she had to say.

"You have to go to Ms. Santos and tell her the truth."

"Yeah, right," Darrell sneered. "Like she's going to believe that the popular jocks have organized a counterfeit ring."

"But they have, right? I want to write the story. In fact"—Sam winced a little—"I already told Mr. Blair I was working on an exposé, but you have to tell Ms. Santos before the story runs, so she can do something about it."

During the long pause, Blaze scratched at the kitchen door. Sam let him in, and the border collie bounded in circles as if he hadn't seen her in days. Sam gave him a dog cookie and ruffled his ears.

"Why do I have to do it? Why can't you?" Darrell asked.

"I won't."

"Do you think she'll tell who ratted on them?" he asked.

"No. I think she'll say she got it from an anonymous source, but you never know about Ms. Santos."

Just a few weeks ago, the principal had kicked her off the bus for no good reason.

"She might ask how you got that pass, though," Sam suggested. "Do you want to tell me?"

As if Darrell had been waiting for her to ask, he blurted,

"Kris gave it to me to shut me up."

Blackmail?

Sam felt even dumber for admiring Kris Cameron. To his credit, Darrell didn't rub it in.

When Sam hung up, they had a deal. Darrell would tell Ms. Santos and Sam would write the story. As she left the kitchen, Sam thought she'd agreed to a bad bargain. If Kris and his football henchmen didn't kill her, Rachel would.

But Sam knew they'd all have to stand in line behind Gram and Dad if she didn't pass algebra.

She trudged toward the stairs. "I'm going back to

solitary confinement," she shouted toward the living room.

"Have fun, dear," Gram called.

Really, sometimes Gram had a completely sick sense of humor.

The storm had turned wet. Clumps of snowflakes smacked Sam's hair as she and Jen got off the school bus the next day. Everything around them was white, except for Gram's car. The yellow Buick labored through the snow, tire chains clinking.

Gram rolled down her window as she stopped, and Sam tugged Jen along with her.

"You'll drive Jen home, too, right?"

"Of course, unless she wants to come with us. Her mother said she could go over to Trudy's to see Faith—"

"Cool!"

"Yes! I can hardly wait!"

"Trudy has nothing in the house to read, and I'm saving her a trip to the Darton library by bringing her a few novels."

Sam had a terrifying vision of Trudy's truck plowing snowdrifts like an insane Christmas sleigh, but she kept it to herself.

"That's nice of you, Gram," she said as she and Jen piled into the backseat.

Five minutes later, they could see Deerpath Ranch. Snow rounded its roof like white sugar icing.

Sam knew she'd thought it looked scary before, but she couldn't quite picture it.

"I haven't forgotten you have a test tomorrow, Samantha, so we won't be long," Gram said.

"Okay," Sam said. Then she remembered her good news. "I don't know how well I did on my English test"—Sam leaned forward to talk to Gram, "but when Miss Finch, that's my English teacher, walked past Mr. Blair's door and caught my eye during sixth period, she smiled and gave me a thumbs-up. That's got to be good, don't you think?"

"Absolutely," Gram said. "But of course I never doubted you."

Sam settled back, feeling tranquil.

Her grades were coming up, so Gram and Dad would be happy. Darrell had talked with Ms. Santos, and she had been disappointed in Kris, but eager to punish him for running the counterfeit ring. The Phantom was fine, probably all cozied down in his secret valley. Life was good.

Even before she climbed out of the car, Sam heard Belle neighing.

"We'll come inside in just a minute, Gram." Sam and Jen headed for the barn. "Poor Belle. Faith pulls her tail," Sam explained. "She's kind of a brat, but you'll love her."

Belle loomed large in the dim barn. She crowded against the stall door and her neigh was deafening.

"It's really dark in here," Sam said. "Let me turn on

the overhead lights." Sam did, and Jen stood on tiptoe, squinting past the mare into the stall. "Faith is so frisky and smart, and she's a Medicine Hat pinto—"

"Could she be in a different stall?" Jen interrupted. Her face glowed sickly pale.

"What? Jen, that's not funny."

Sam stormed past her friend and looked into the stall for herself.

Belle was all alone.

Chapter Eighteen ॐ

THEY WASTED NO TIME. Sam and Jen made a quick but complete search for tracks that weren't there. They jogged through the corrals and looked in corners of the ranch yard. All the while, Belle neighed for her baby.

"We've got to go after her," Sam said. Then she and Jen ran for the house.

Like a bad dream, the snow slowed their feet. Ahead, the house windows glinted gold in the dull afternoon. With each step they seemed to get farther away, not closer.

If Faith had been in her stall, they'd be going inside to drink tea and eat cookies. If Faith hadn't vanished, Sam would feel as peaceful as she had in Gram's backseat. Minutes ago, all had been right with the world, but now Faith was gone.

If she wasn't found soon, she would die.

"Faith's gone!" Sam shouted as they burst through the door.

Gram held a teapot in one hand. It wavered, and for a minute, Sam thought she'd drop it. She didn't, but Trudy set a plate of cookies on the table and sank into a chair. For one horrible minute, Sam thought Trudy would collapse.

"How could she be gone?" Trudy asked. "Is the mare—"

"Belle's there. It's like the stall door closed her inside and Faith slipped through the fence or something. I don't know, but we need to find her before dark."

It might already be too late. Sam thought of the river, of gulches and gullies and rumors about cougars, bears, and packs of feral dogs.

"Mrs. Allen," Jen said, polishing the lenses of her glasses, which had fogged up in the warm kitchen, "can we borrow some jeans? Sam and I will ride two of your horses and start searching."

"Not alone, you won't," Trudy started, but Gram touched her arm.

"They're good, strong riders. If we had more saddle horses, we could all go."

"Judge isn't up to it," Trudy admitted. "And neither am I . . . so, all right." She nodded.

"I'll call Wyatt and the Elys." Gram moved toward the phone.

"My dad's home, too," Jen said. "He'll go."

Having a big search party would help, but Faith's pale coat would act like camouflage, and she couldn't avoid even the most obvious hazards. Sam felt a wave of despair wash over her.

"She's so little." Sam covered her mouth with one gloved hand.

"No lost causes." Trudy's voice was harsh. "Isn't that what you told me, girl?"

Sam fought off stinging tears and tried to catch her breath. Then she nodded.

"There'll be plenty of time to cry later, if we have to," Trudy said. She hurried to the stairs, talking over her shoulder. "I'll get you some clothes, then you can take Calico and Ginger. Those tough old girls will do their best for you."

Fifteen minutes later, Sam and Jen were dressed in layers of ill-fitting clothes and mounted on the pinto mares.

While they were saddling up, Sam had found the saddlebags she'd forgotten in a corner of the barn two days ago.

As much as she hated the thought of Faith's being injured, the first aid supplies inside her saddlebags might come in handy.

She didn't take the time to unload the camera. If it should break during this search, well, Faith was more important.

"You girls stay together," Gram ordered. "Don't split up unless you're with Wyatt or Jake or one of the others. They're on their way."

"Okay, Gram," Sam said, but she was looking around the ranch yard, trying to think like Faith.

Belle's cries surrounded them.

"Should we let her out and follow her?" Jen asked.

Sam had been wondering the same thing. "I don't think so," she said. "I've watched them, and Faith does better on her own. When she's trying to obey Belle, she doesn't pay attention to anything but her mama's voice."

"That makes sense," Jen said. "I hate the thought of her out there all alone."

Sam swung Calico toward the lane. "That's why we've got to find her."

An hour later, the snow had stopped falling, but if there'd been tiny hoofprints in the snow, the wind had erased them.

"I can't see anything," Jen said.

"Jake might. He's an awfully good tracker."

"I hope so, but look." Jen pointed at the horizon.

The sun looked cold and gray as a dropped nickel and it was about to set. When it did, the temperature would plummet. And more snow waited in the white-bellied clouds.

"It's nearly dusk and we haven't seen anything. We need a plan," Jen said.

Sam tried to think, but it was awfully hard. Wind

blasted through her clothes, chilling her arms and legs. The range lay in cold white sweeps around them. The Calico Mountains rose in pale jagged peaks ahead. This wilderness hid entire bands of wild horses. One tiny foal would disappear like a single snowflake.

Faith didn't have much of a chance, but if they gave up, she'd have none.

"I don't think she'll head for the mountains," Sam said, pointing at blue shadows amid the snowdrifts. "It'll be slick in the shadows, and she'd have a hard time climbing. If she's still walking, she'll head where the footing is easiest."

Jen nodded, but they both knew a tired baby might lie down and sleep.

"The visibility's great," Jen said. "If she could see . . . "

"She can't, but we can see each other," Sam said. "If we split up, but keep each other in sight, we'd cover twice as much area."

Neither of them mentioned their promise to Gram—or every rule they'd been taught about snow safety.

"If I go that way, I'll be on Deerpath land, but I'll be riding parallel to Three Ponies Ranch," Jen said. "If it's all the same to you, I don't want to meet up with Jake. So, you go that way, and I'll head back along the road."

"Okay. We need to check the base of every sage-brush and piñon big enough to shelter her, too."

A gust of wind howled between them, stirring snow into a white whirlwind. Sam let it die down before she continued.

"And we've got to keep each other in sight. If the wind comes up like that much more, we can't stay separate, right?"

"Right," Jen said.

Calico didn't question Sam's orders to weave among the sagebrush and rocks. She backed and turned, tolerating each interruption as Sam twisted in the saddle to wave at Jen and wait for her answering motion.

Sam's nose was cold. She wished someone would appear in front of her and say Faith had been found, everything was all right, and she could go home and crawl into bed.

"Horse angels," Sam murmured. "Tell me you've seen them before, Calico, because we need one tonight."

Calico nickered and Sam saw something.

"That's no angel," Sam told the mare, "but thanks anyway."

Only Jake rode a black horse with a mane crested like a Mohawk. No one else radiated anger through layers of insulated clothes.

Jake pulled Witch to a stop about five feet from Calico. Powdered with snow, his Stetson had turned white. His brown eyes blazed from beneath its brim.

"You know this is an idiot thing to do."

"I know Faith will be glad to have you rescue her, even if you think it's a waste of time."

"I'm not doing it for Faith."

Jake's breath hung in the air and both horses stood still. Then he pointed past her.

"Your partner in crime is swinging her arms around like she's trying to flag down a train," he said. "Wave back."

"So she won't think you're about to strangle me?"

"It would be a good guess," Jake said. "Just wave."

Sam swiveled in her saddle, returned Jen's wave, and watched her go back to searching.

"I'm on my way to the ranch," Jake said. "I'll look for tracks before the light's entirely gone."

"But the wind—"

"I'll do what I can, okay?" Jake snapped. "Now, where are you headed? Your dad and Pepper are trailering horses in as far as Deerpath. I'm meeting them there, and I want to report where you were last seen."

Witch's black muzzle snaked out to nip at Calico.

Squealing, the pinto swerved and the saddlebags flapped, giving her a thump because of the camera's weight.

The camera.

Wild horses.

What had Trudy said that night when Sam had yearned to photograph wild horses in the dark?

"Sam? Don't space out on me," Jake ordered.

"Wait." She held up one hand, trying to think past the cold. "Okay, got it." She looked up at Jake. "It's a real long shot," she told him, "but Trudy said sometimes mustangs go to the hot springs. It's not far."

"How deep—?" Jake's jaw snapped shut before he finished the question. He shook his head. "Brat, that's more than a long shot."

Sam wheeled Calico in a spray of snow and kicked her into a clumsy lope. Behind her, Jake shouted something. Sam didn't stop to ask him what, but it sounded like *Good luck*.

She didn't have to tell Jen that she had an idea. At Sam's galloping approach, Jen reined Ginger after Calico. The two pinto mares scattered snow with such energy, they seemed to be having fun.

Please let Faith be there, Sam thought. *Please let her be safe and warm.*

Stray snowflakes stuck to Sam's eyelashes. She hoped it was snow stirred by the wind, but when she looked up, she saw the storm was closing in again.

No matter how fast she rode, the flakes clung to her cheeks, but she didn't dare take a hand from her reins to rub them off.

Off to the right, Sam saw the tree house. The land underfoot sloped and she saw tall brush up ahead. Trudy had said the hot springs was surrounded by reeds.

Calico passed Ginger. Head up, nostrils distended, her gait became a flat run. Sam couldn't have guessed the mare had such speed.

Calico knew each dip and rise on this plain. The smooth rhythm of her gait made Sam feel like the world's best rider. All at once, the mare slowed. Her gallop changed to a prance.

"Hey, Jen!" Sam twisted in the saddle. Wrong direction. She turned around the other way. "Jen?"

A curtain of white swept across Sam and Calico, wrapping them in wind-driven snow. Once it passed, Sam saw they were alone. Calico had outrun Ginger all right, and Jen was nowhere to be seen.

Chapter Nineteen ❧

$\mathcal{T}$HE WASTELAND AROUND her might as well have been the Arctic. Sam couldn't see a fence, the ranch lights, or even the tall tree that held the tree house.

Snow swarmed like gnats before her eyes. The west wind that had been at her back all afternoon was joined by gusts from many directions. Flickering flakes turned into long whips of snow lashing at her from every side.

Ahead, she caught a glimpse of brush wearing shawls of snow. The plants grew steadily taller, then ended in a thicket of trees. Sam couldn't even tell what kind of trees they were. Maybe pines, but they looked round as snowballs.

She headed for them. Vegetation meant water.

And then the trees were hidden by the snow shafts. She tried to make sense of their dancing. They shifted and cut to her right. Then, just when she thought she could see past them, they blurred, dissolved, and reformed to her left.

She pressed a palm on Calico's hindquarters, steadying herself to look behind. No tracks. She leaned back farther. Even at the horse's heels, she could see no hoofmarks in the snow. Not even Jake could find her, Sam thought. Just then, a million fused flakes hit her face, threatening to suffocate her.

She wiped them off with her gloved hand.

Get a grip. You know this land.

She'd ridden it for all but two years of her life. She should be able to ride out of this place as confidently as she'd ridden in.

She could always count on the Calico Mountains as a true landmark. If she rode away from them, she'd come to the river. Once she crossed it, she'd be near home. But even the mountains were hidden by blowing snow.

Calico shifted, wanting to move off, but Sam kept her still. If she let Calico have her head, the mare might take her farther away from the ranches.

Lost and alone—wasn't that what her mother had feared most for her child? Well, her mom's worst nightmare had come true.

Sam sat a minute, letting the words run around in her mind. They should be scary, but she wasn't afraid. Not yet. She knew the range, and so did Calico. They'd be all right.

"That doesn't mean I couldn't use some help," Sam said aloud. She couldn't have said who she talked to, and her voice sounded so small, that she fell silent.

Sam listened and heard nothing beyond the screaming wind. No hooves ran after her. No trucks crunched over the snow. She couldn't even hear tires on the highway, which couldn't be that far off.

"Let's see if we can find those trees," she shouted to Calico. She'd seen them just a few minutes ago, so she clucked to Calico, loosed the reins, and hoped for the best.

Even if they missed the springs and Faith, she had to stay by those trees. She knew how to build a shelter against the snow, and it looked like she was going to need one.

"There they are," she said, but quietly. Her mind might be fashioning blowing clots of snow into what she wanted to see, not what was really there.

She reined Calico hard right, and the mare fought the change in direction. Crow-hopping and snorting, Calico wanted to go uphill. At least it felt like uphill. The mare lunged and skidded.

"Fall on your face if you want," Sam muttered, "but I'm not going down with you."

Sam would bet the mare couldn't understand her words. Cold seemed to have frozen the joints of her jaw. But Calico would understand pressure, so Sam used her weight and every ounce of strength in her legs to direct the mare.

Grudgingly, Calico went.

The pinto had turned completely white. Her mane wore so much snow, it fractured and fell off in sheets as she battled Sam.

The trees were there. They didn't hold the tree house or surround the hot springs, but three pine trees stood in a half ring, perfect for the snow shelter Sam could build.

If she had the nerve to dismount. Calico seemed to have calmed down, but Sam's hands were so cold and her gloves so soaked, she was afraid she might lose her grip on the reins.

Not if she had dry gloves. Sam urged the mare close to the trees. Once they were underneath, Sam looked up at the dark undersides of the branches.

"This is better, isn't it, girl?" Sam asked.

She hoped Calico would appreciate the protection enough to stand still. Sam brushed the snow from her saddlebags, unbuckled them, and slipped out her fresh gloves.

Had the wind developed teeth of ice? That's what it felt like in the minutes she struggled into the dry gloves. But then her fingers were warm and relief made her brave.

"I'm tying you to this low branch and you're not going anywhere," Sam said as she swung to the ground. She stumbled on the uneven footing and the snow squeaked, but the mare didn't try to bolt.

Sam's hands were clumsy as she tied the horse to a low branch, but the knot looked okay. Three trees didn't make much shelter, but the mare seemed to know it was better than nothing.

Calico clamped her tail against her hindquarters, turning away from the wind, and that's when Sam noticed the torrents of snow had slacked off. The wind came from the west again, and it was quieter. Maybe . . .

"I'm not going to be fooled," she insisted as she stared at the trees. "I'm going to make a little hut anyway."

She kicked snow from the ground and found two fallen branches that were long enough to form the roof of a shelter. That wasn't nearly enough, so she stripped two low branches from the trees.

It had been a long time since her sixth grade winter survival class, but she knew how to use the existing branches as supports for other sticks you angled in there like shelves.

She explained all this to Calico, but the mare closed her eyes and flattened her ears. She was not happy.

"That makes a roof," Sam told her, just the same. "Then, I'll have to look for pine needles and other stuff to put between the branches, so it doesn't leak snow all over me. By that time, my gloves will be soaked again."

Unsympathetic, Calico moved to the end of her tethered rein. Disturbed by the pull, snow sifted down from the upper branches onto Sam.

With numb hands, she brushed it off. Before she got busy building, she'd need to move the mare and tie her somewhere else. Otherwise, Calico could destroy the whole shelter with a single lunge.

Sam yawned and rubbed her arms. The wind hushed to a whisper. Then it was quiet. Somewhere, snow slid from branches and fell with a plop. It must be getting warmer, but it sure wasn't warm enough.

With something like hunger, she thought of the matches in her saddlebags and wondered if these soggy pine needles would act as tinder. If so, could she peel off pieces of bark that weren't too wet to burn?

"Finish the stupid roof first!" Sam's words came out garbled, but loud in the windless quiet, and this time Calico bolted.

The clumsily tied rein jerked loose and the mare took off at a trot.

"No! Calico, come back!"

Staggering through the deep drifts, Sam followed. She had to hurry. Even though the mare had to lift her hooves high, almost prancing to make progress, she was drawing away fast.

Neck arched, Calico advanced into the unearthly quiet, then shattered it by nickering like a young mare.

She stopped when she gave the nicker, and Sam didn't let the opportunity slip past. The only way she could reach that trailing rein now was to fling herself forward, as if tackling it.

She did, then gripped the reins tight as she stood.

Calico showed no sign of trying to get away. Snow fell again, sifting down like powdered sugar, but Sam didn't feel as cold as before.

Panting, she stood with one hand on the mare's shoulder, listening in the direction the mare's ears pointed.

"What is it, girl? Do you see Faith?" Sam knew she'd have a better chance of seeing if she were mounted.

She swung into the saddle, then leaned low, trying to match her field of vision with the mare's. But Calico must have heard something, or smelled it, because nothing moved.

Or maybe something did. Sam blinked. A wavery mist showed through the brush. It must be a hot spring.

All at once, it was just there. Calico had walked right to it, and the small pool looked so warm and inviting, Sam feared she was hallucinating.

Had Calico been trying to come here all along? Sam decided that was a distinct possibility.

"Sorry, girl," she said, but the mare's ears didn't flicker to catch her voice. Calico was intent on something that had nothing to do with her rider.

Sam could barely see through the steam rising to meet the falling snow. She urged the mare forward. She went, stiff-legged and slow, then stopped again.

A stand of trees stood like icicles across the pool.

Just feet ahead of Sam was the blind foal.

"Faith!"

Knee-deep in bluish water, the filly swung her Medicine Hat head from side to side. Her grateful squeals had Sam scrambling down, still holding Calico's reins so the mare wouldn't escape. It got warmer as she walked forward. The nightmarish cold didn't exist in this tiny, sheltered place.

Satisfied that she was safe, Faith bucked and splashed. Her antics made another horse toss his watchful head.

Half hidden by mist, silver against the white trees, the Phantom stood on the far side of the pool. Motionless except for the wind in his mane and tail, he watched.

"So there is a horse angel, after all," Sam whispered.

The stallion's snort created a cloud around his face.

Sam knew stallions often killed foals that were not their own, but Zanzibar had been guarding Faith.

Faith took a hesitant step, walking into her darkness. The brave little filly was ready to go home, but Sam wanted to stay all night to watch the Phantom.

The stallion's ears swiveled and his head jerked up. Another horse crunched across the snow.

She knew she should call out. It must be Jen. But the Phantom showed no sign of bolting and Sam didn't want to miss a minute with him.

Even after Jake had hit him and Sam had shouted at him, the stallion had forgiven her. Sam refused to send him away again, even if Jen passed by, leaving her behind.

"Zanzibar," she whispered. "Stay with me a minute."

The stallion sighed. The exhalation relaxed his entire body. His tense neck bowed and his weight shifted forward, greeting her. He nickered and struck the ground with one hoof, giving the foal a snort to quiet her when she fretted.

Through the misty darkness, Sam watched the stallion toss his head. Forelock and mane stirred a flurry of steam and snowflakes, and they curled around him in magic currents. He might have been a unicorn beside enchanted waters. But he wasn't. He was Zanzibar and he was hers.

All at once, the stallion lifted his head and neighed.

Calico answered and then another horse called from nearby. If she'd had to guess, she'd say the rasping sound came from Witch. But Jake wouldn't have come back.

And if he had, Sam thought, swallowing, she didn't want to see him.

Held silent by the mustang's trust, Sam didn't move or call out. She didn't turn to look at the approaching horse and rider, because the Phantom might vanish before she turned back.

And so, she watched him go. The Phantom slipped through the trees on the far side of the hot springs.

Calico whinnied her despair and gathered herself to bolt after him. It was tough to handle her from the ground, but Sam fought with the mare. Finally, she gave a sharp jerk on the reins.

"You're scaring Faith," she said, rubbing the mare's neck. "And you're acting like he's a rock star or something." Calico gave a low nicker and Sam could only hope the horse had regained her good sense. "Although, I kind of know what you mean."

Sam stared at the spot where the Phantom had been just minutes ago.

"Hey!" the rider called. It was Jake.

"We're here," Sam called back.

"Who the heck is *we*?" Jake grumbled as he rode into the clearing surrounding the hot springs. "I just passed Jen."

"Me, Calico, and baby Faith." Sam's spirits soared as she looked up at him. "If you just passed Jen, why were you coming back?"

A glare stronger than words told her to hush, but Sam didn't. "I thought you were going to read tracks."

Jake shrugged as if he was only being sensible. "I had a hunch you'd get yourself into trouble."

"A hunch? You mean one of those things level-headed guys don't believe in because they can't see them with their own eyes?"

"You know"—Jake pointed an index finger covered with heavy leather gloves—"Witch has had enough of playin' in the snow. I could turn her toward home and leave you to wrestle that filly up on your saddle alone. How about that?"

She knew he wouldn't.

He swung out of the saddle and slapped Witch's reins into Sam's hand.

"Hold on to her and get back on that paint. I'll hand you the foal." He turned to wade through the deep snow.

He was being bossy because he was embarrassed. Just the same, Sam stuck out her tongue at his back.

She saw him look down at the foal and shake his head. He mumbled something, and Sam would bet he didn't particularly like the idea of getting wet. But he bent his knees, and the snow covering the back of his jacket was suddenly crisscrossed with lines.

"Here we go," he said quietly. Water swished and he straightened. When he lifted the foal, Sam heard no splashing or fussing. Faith didn't struggle, but Sam saw a tiny gold muzzle rest on the shoulder of Jake's leather coat.

Jake grunted and moved, getting a good grip on the filly before he turned.

"This little gal is tryin' to work me," Jake muttered. "Tell her I've got no use for silly mustangs who wander away from their mamas."

He turned then, stamping his boots in the snow so that he didn't slip with the foal. He was still grumbling, but as Jake staggered toward Sam, he was smiling.

Perfect. Inspiration flashed like lightning and Sam grabbed for the saddlebags.

Trusting the horses to stay ground-tied, Sam made her cold fingers fly. She unbuckled the flap and retrieved her camera. She eased it from its nest of socks, and before Jake could frown or protest, she fired off three shots of the cowboy and the fragile, long-legged foal.

"You're crazy as a bedbug if you think I won't pay you back for that," Jake said. "What kinda picnic is this, that you're taking pictures instead of helping?" He kept his voice low because of Faith, but he was irritated.

Sam didn't care. He'd get over his aggravation.

She'd already started congratulating herself on winning the Night Magic competition when Witch protested her nearness to Calico.

The two mares squealed. Sam kept her grip on the camera as she grabbed for both sets of reins. She caught Witch, but Calico's reins ran through her fingers. Escaping Witch's snapping teeth, the paint headed for home.

It was quiet for a minute before Jake sighed and shook his head. "Leave it to a female to pay back a good deed with trouble."

"You'd better be talking about Calico," Sam said.

"Sure. 'Course I am." Jake hefted the foal a little higher in his arms. "You make the next plan, Brat, because Witch doesn't carry double. Ever."

Ten minutes later, Witch proved Jake wrong.

Jake sat in front, holding the reins and Faith, while Sam sat behind.

Sam should have been miserable. Snowflakes pelted her hair and dripped, melting down her neck. Her arms cramped where they circled Jake's waist.

Still, Sam sighed with contentment. She imagined the eyes of a silver stallion, watching her out of sight, and she had never been happier in her life.

From
Phantom Stallion
∞ 6 ∞
THE CHALLENGER

"Oh, my gosh." Sam took a breath, then pointed. "Look."

A tall black horse strutted apart from the herd. It was Moon. Sam was sure of it. She'd just recognized him when a movement farther up caught her eyes.

Through a piñon-choked pass, Sam saw a pale flicker. And there—dust floated in the wake of something moving fast. The stallion raced toward the intruder.

"Is that his son?" Brynna asked.

Sam nodded. "That's New Moon."

Moon shoved into the herd of mustangs, scattering bays and sorrels, mares and foals.

"He's sure not trying to be sneaky about it," Brynna said. "Every horse down there can see he's trying to cut out that blood bay mare."

Hooves clattered on rock. Ace and Jeep shifted uneasily at the Phantom's warning neigh.

Sam turned toward Brynna, who looked at her with raised eyebrows.

"Stallions do a lot of pretending," Brynna said. "I've always heard they don't fight unless they must."

"I don't know," Sam said. "I think Moon's pushed his father too far."

As if Moon heard Sam's worry, he let the blood bay return to the other mares. He whirled to face his sire.

Sam and Brynna rode a little closer, drawing rein at a relatively flat spot where bare aspen stood tall and white. Here, Jeep and Ace could stand together, and they could all watch.

The Phantom stopped about ten feet from his son and laid his ears back. Any horse could read the stallion's irritation, but Moon didn't move away.

The Phantom stamped a front hoof. He looked impatient, but Moon switched his tail as if he didn't care.

He's asking for it, Sam thought.

Still, the stallion didn't treat Moon like a challenger. Lowering his silvery head, the Phantom bared his teeth and snaked his neck in the scolding, herding move he'd use on any mare or foal that disobeyed.

For a second, Moon hesitated. His head turned slightly. His lips moved, as if chewing over the problem of his father's strength. His tail drooped and he glanced at the mares.

All at once, wind raced through the canyon. Its scent carried reminders of the days Moon had ruled these mares.

Inky torrents of mane flew around Moon's head and neck. He bobbed his head, higher every time, refusing to be scolded. Neck arched, tail flung high, he defied his father by refusing to retreat.

Moon didn't know what he was getting into. Even though he stood taller than his sire, the Phantom had the broad chest and thick muscles of a mature stallion.

"This is all play-acting," Brynna reassured Sam. "Stallions don't want to draw blood. Even if he's a sure winner—like the Phantom—he could be hurt. He knows even a small injury might make him slower. And that would be bad for the herd."

"You didn't see him fight Hammer," Sam said. "When Hammer didn't back down, the Phantom was all over him."

Sam would never forget the loud and brutal fight. Both stallions had been streaked with blood.

The Phantom gave Moon time to size him up while Sam and Brynna watched in silence.

The horses stood still for so long, Sam noticed the shiny rocks around them. They must have worn a skim of ice earlier, but now it had melted off. The smell of wet earth wasn't flowery like it was in spring. Autumn was ending and winter was nearly here.

Sam took turns holding her reins with one hand while she tucked the other under the warmth of her jacket.

Time's up. With a jerk of his head, the Phantom signaled his son to fight or flee.

The silver stallion approached like a king. Moon

fidgeted, but he held his ground until the Phantom stood in front of him. The horses stood eye-to-eye, then the Phantom moved forward, giving his son's forehead a shove.

Moon retreated a step and the Phantom came after him, jostling his head again.

All at once, Moon reacted like a teenager who'd been pushed too far. With a high-pitched squeal, the black rose up on his hind legs. The silver stallion must have known what would happen, because he reared at exactly the same instant.

For a moment, they stood liked mirrored reflections, one dark and one light.

The Phantom dodged past the black's threshing forelegs, ducking to grab his mane. He tugged, pulling the black off balance, then dodging out of the way.

Moon fell, but he bolted up at once. Looking anxious, he trotted a circle around his father, but Sam could see he'd skinned his knees.

"He sparred with Yellowtail and Spike and he always won," Sam said.

"Who?"

"A bay and a chestnut in his bachelor band. Mrs. Coley named them. We saw them play-fighting once, and Moon was clearly the best. I think he's confused because the Phantom's not such an easy opponent."

"Look at the mares," Brynna said.

The Phantom's herd grazed, unconcerned. When Moon gave a series of short snorts, the mares looked up, but they knew the outcome of the fight. They were indifferent about how the Phantom won.

All but the blood bay. The mare Moon had tried to steal seemed interested. Searching for a better view, she stepped away from the herd.

Sudden hoofbeats made Sam look back to the stallions.

"He's giving it another try," Sam said.

Suddenly, Moon darted toward the Phantom. Ears pinned, head flat, he grabbed for the gray. The Phantom swerved, but the smear of foam on his neck showed how close Moon had come to biting him.

"Too close," Brynna said. "Now the Phantom's getting mad."

Sam heard Brynna swallow, and there was something about her nervousness that made Sam glad. They both knew battles like this had been acted out for centuries, but neither could accept this one as no big deal.

The fight turned loud as the stallions changed tactics. Hooves skittered, then hammered on hide as they launched powerful kicks with their hind legs. Guttural neighs were wrenched from both horses.

The blood bay mare trotted closer, but she didn't get far. The lead mare drove her back with the others.

Distracted by the skirmish between the lead mare and the blood bay, Moon's head swung away from the Phantom.

The silver stallion charged.

Surprised, Moon broke into a reluctant run. From above, it looked to Sam like there was only one way out of the canyon. Scored with red scratches and gouges, Moon galloped toward it.

When the tiger dun lead mare joined in the pursuit, the Phantom stopped, letting her take over.

The stallion trotted around his herd, circling again and again.

"He's counting to make sure they're all there," Brynna joked, but her words were breathy, as if she was unsettled by what might have happened.

Suddenly a low, angry squeal made Sam look toward Moon. "It's not over." She gasped.

Moon refused to be driven out by the dun mare. He wheeled at a run and came charging back.

"Why doesn't he just quit?" Sam demanded.

"He's braver than he is smart," Brynna said.

The Phantom must have expected Moon's stubbornness, because he ran toward him at full speed. Sam drew a shaky breath.

"If he goes down, it's all over, isn't it." Brynna's words weren't really a question.

Sam knew Brynna was right. If Moon fell and the Phantom attacked, the younger stallion could be killed.